'It's shoot-to-~~~~~~~~~~~~~~~~~~~~~~~~~ the deadliest crit~~~~~~~~~~~~~~~~~~~~~~~r it's you. Go for it, snoot on sight! Speed up, and let's get this war over! Remember... if you don't get it, it will get *you*!'

... Meanwhile, Number Five was having a think, huddled up in the centre of the road.

Short Circuit

a Novel by Colin Wedgelock

from the screenplay by Steve Wilson

Sphere Books Limited

Sphere Books Limited
27 Wrights Lane, London W8 5TZ

First published in Great Britain by
Sphere Books Ltd 1986
Copyright © 1986 Tri-Star Pictures, Inc. and PSO Presentations

Short Circuit is a trademark of
Tri-Star Pictures, Inc. and PSO
Presentations. All Rights Reserved.

TRADE
MARK

Set in Plantin

Printed and bound in Great Britain by
Cox & Wyman Ltd., Reading

Chapter 1

It was a drowsy day, heat rolling in from the sun-baked hills that surrounded the shallow valley. The air was thick and humid, its quietude a deceptive calm, the sort that threatens violent change. It was a day for ice-cooled drinks and a shady awning beside a swimming pool or on a beach, but here in the Oregon heights, simmering in the static heatwave, the only reprieve from the sun's furnace was in the mind: a hope that this would not take long. The assembled dignitaries sat uncomfortably on the wooden bleachers, the ladies fanning themselves with their white card invitations, the men, most of them in uniform, sitting stiffly with hands on military knees, trying to keep their arms away from the sides of their bodies to delay that moment when sweat patches would begin, inevitably, to darken their uniform jackets.

Thunder rolled ominously somewhere in the hills, and a few of the guests looked up expectantly. A sudden downpour would bring this delayed and unexplained event to a swift conclusion. But although there were clouds, dark and tall and full of elemental might, they were a long way away.

The white sun beat down on the tranquil field. Poppies, bright red and bursting with seed, nodded in the few vestiges of breeze that reached them.

On a small raised platform in front of the makeshift grandstand, an anxious-looking man in a summer-weight suit stood with his hand on a telephone installed beside a lectern. This was Dr. Howard Marner, President of the corporation that occupied the sprawling concrete complex adjacent to the field. The telephone rang suddenly, a discreet, almost silent beeping noise. With movements of exaggerated calm Dr. Marner picked up the receiver.

'Yes,' he said. 'Yes ... yes ... yes.' Holding the phone to

1

his ear he turned to look at the waiting audience. Every single one of them was staring at him. 'Yes,' he said again, forcing a smile. 'Good.'

He replaced the receiver, and turned to gaze out across the field.

Nothing happened.

Bees droned, the long grass waved flaccidly, an unseen bird made a curious noise, like a high-pitched cough. White invitations fluttered, and beads of perspiration rolled with the utmost good manners down the necks of important men.

The knuckles of Dr. Marner's hands, resting on the lectern in front of him, were as white as the chalky dust that had drifted over from the parking lot a hundred yards away.

There was another ominous rumbling in the distance, and a second wave of anticipation ran through the audience. One of the ladies held out an expectant hand, hoping for the first drop of rain.

But on the far side of the field, behind a clump of trees, oily black smoke rose in a billowing column. After a moment another appeared, drifting up into the sticky air. Soon waves of sound flooded across the field, as one great engine after another roared into life.

Dr. Marner turned again to his audience, a sickly grin spreading over his under-developed, almost adolescent features. But now there was no one looking at him. They were all staring at the far side of the field.

Trundling into view, slowly at first, but with increasing momentum as they lumbered into full speed, came an armoured column, clanking and gleaming, bouncing heavily over ruts, churning up the soil and vegetation in a brown cloud of careless destruction.

At the head of the column were three front-line main battle tanks, the barrels of their nuclear cannons pointed straight at the waiting audience. Behind them, line abreast, were two armoured missile launchers, their ground-to-air ABMs already canted for action. Two more battle tanks

2

followed, then behind them were three armoured personnel carriers.

Already, the vehicles at the front of the column had wheeled to one side, and were deploying themselves on three sides of the watching, and increasingly impressed, audience. The turrets of the tanks, auto-controlled, kept a steady bead on the crowd.

Sun glinted on blue-black steel, and there was a smell of oil and smoke. Already pouring into the field from behind the trees were several troop-carriers, the foot-soldiers sitting in the back, lurching with the violent motions of the trucks, the straps of their helmets swinging around their jaws, their automatic rifles held ready for action.

It seemed there was no end to the column of deadly weaponry pouring into the field. The tanks that had arrived first were now speeding to and fro in an impressive display of nastiness, the cannon turrets holding steady, the great bulk of the machines bouncing and lurching, the caterpillar treads setting up a clattering and screeching that seemed to shake the air.

The most senior of the military men stood up for a better view, his lips quivering with excitement. Taking his cue, the others leapt to attention around him. Blue eyes glittered proudly at this sight of undoubted might. When Uncle Sam kicked ass, he went out and kicked ass in the biggest and best way.

The ladies, their fluttering invitations stilled, also stood up, because now they no longer had a clear view.

In the space of under thirty seconds the tranquil pasture had been turned into an arena of military might. Not content with mere display, the tanks now started manoeuvring cleverly around each other, battlefield tactics to the fore.

Into the heart of this mêlée, apparently from nowhere, although probably from some concealed trench in the middle of the field, hurtled a small object. It was so tiny, and moved so fast, that at first few people noticed it.

Dr. Marner's shoulders straightened, and sun glinted off the thinning patch on the back of his head.

In the swirling clouds of dirt and fragmented grass it was difficult to see clearly. The new arrival seemed to be a glistening streak of metal, darting around the lumbering tanks with all the fleet delicacy of a scampering ballet dancer.

It came to a halt twenty yards in front of the audience ... but before they could register what it was, or what it really looked like, it sprang into action.

With barely a visible motion, it sprayed the field with darting red beams of laser light. It ducked, dashed to the side, let off another volley. It hurtled back again to the other side, squirted deadly light ... but its work had all been done with the first burst.

Almost as if synchronized, every single battle machine exploded with a violent concussion. The noise clouted the dumbstruck audience like the side of a wall.

The turret of one of the tanks spun into the air like a flipped coin ...

The caterpillar track of one of the personnel carriers careered snakily across the grass ...

A cannon barrel twisted through space like a caber ...

A million shards of armour plate sliced through the shrieking air ...

A tyre from one of the trucks, engulfed in flames, shot like the star of a roman candle, straight up, straight down, trailing black smoke.

And the soldiers flew in all directions, all in pieces. Legs and arms went flailing. Heads rolled and bounced. One body, still intact, flew head-first into the glowing fireball of what had been until two seconds before an armoured missile launcher. Rifles clattered and fell like skittles ...

A helmet, thankfully without a head inside it, rolled like tumbleweed towards the audience. It came to a halt upside down, the strap swinging to and fro.

Then, after everything else had fallen to the ground in a

4

scrapyard of ruin, the petals of the poppies came drifting down, a blood-red snowfall, the eternal witnesses to battle and death, gentle and sinister.

Dr. Marner turned to face his audience.

They were silent, stunned, aghast. The generals stared with blank eyes; the ladies loooked at the multitude of broken bodies.

Dr. Marner could not restrain a smile . . . and it broadened into a grin of happiness as, with considerable delicacy, a ripple of polite applause was accorded him.

Modestly, he inclined his head, then stepped away from his podium and went to where the severed arm of a soldier lay in the grass.

He picked it up, waggled what remained of the elbow to and fro, and a short but quite distinct groan of disappointment was emitted by the crowd.

The arm was made of plaster.

Chapter 2

'Enemy neutralized, ladies and gentlemen. Objective completed.'

The voice was tinny and unwavering, and it carried clearly on the dusty air. Attention shifted from Dr. Marner to the small metallic contraption that was rolling forward from out of the swirling debris just a few yards behind.

Dr. Marner seized a microphone from the lectern.

'Senators, Generals, ladies ... and gentlemen!' he said proudly. 'Meet the star performer!' He held out his free hand, and the contraption came to a halt at his side. 'Okay Chigger,' Marner said.

Around at the side of the bleachers a perspiring young man in a suit was sitting before a portable computer console. On Marner's instruction, he jabbed at a key, and on each side of the grandstand two huge banners rapidly unfurled. NOVA ROBOTICS! TOMORROW IS HERE! The audience barely had time to absorb this difficult concept before Dr. Marner was speaking again.

'Ladies and gentlemen,' he said. 'You have just seen a demonstration, a *successful* demonstration, of S.A.I.N.T. Yes, the Strategic Artificially Intelligent Nuclear Transport. The name of the game is survival, ladies and gentlemen, and S.A.I.N.T. is the key to that game! Nova Robotics is proud to present what is, quite simply, the most sophisticated robot on Earth.'

Now the dust was beginning to settle, the audience could at last see clearly.

The centre of attention was a small robot. It stood on, or was propelled by, two lightweight caterpillar tracks. Its torso was a stocky barrel, misshapen and purely functional, and from this extended two prehensile arms, multi-jointed,

6

fashioned from glinting metal, and each capped with mechanical hands. The 'head' rose from the top of the torso on a telescopic 'neck'; its most prominent feature was a twin lens arrangement giving an uncanny impression of eyes.

If it had not just single-handedly destroyed what seemed to be half an army, it could easily have been dismissed as a flimsy toy.

The audience regarded it respectfully.

Still at the microphone, Dr. Marner said theatrically, 'Say, Number One, I'm feeling awfully thirsty. I sure could use a gin and tonic ... on the rocks.'

The robot went into action. One of its arms reached into the shaded area beneath the platform and brought out a small tray. On this had already been placed two bottles, a lime, a swizzle-stick, a glass ... and a huge block of ice.

'Ladies and gentlemen, I ask you to watch this closely. The manipulators are capable not only of incredible strength' – the robot lifted the block of ice in one hand and crushed it effortlessly – 'but extreme delicacy too' – while at the same time it picked up the glass, and held it under the ice to catch the fragments as they fell. 'High density silicon chips ...'

Marner droned on technically, while his thirsty audience watched the robot. It moved with all the precision of a practised bartender, pouring a shot of gin over the ice, then fizzing in a measure of clear tonic water. A razor-sharp blade, extruded from one of its hands, sliced the lime expertly, and a wedge was plopped into the drink. The final touches were a piece of lime peel, twisted zestily over the lip of the glass, and three swift swirls with the swizzle-stick.

As the robot held the drink out to its master, misty condensation was already forming on the walls of the glass.

'... point five spacing,' Dr. Marner was saying, 'and full three-dimensional human simulatory sight through not only the visible spectra but in infra-red and ultraviolet too.'

He took the drink absent-mindedly, and placed it carelessly on the lectern.

'Well, Number One,' he said. 'You want to finish that model airplane you got for your birthday?' Almost before he had finished speaking, the robot had produced a large cardboard box from somewhere. Inside was one of those plastic aircraft assembly kits, requiring cement, paint, and hours of patience.

The metal hands blurred into action. Within a matter of two or three seconds the model airplane was finished ... assembled, cemented and painted in the standard silvery finish of the Soviet Air Force.

'The registration number, ladies and –' But they were intent on what the robot was doing. Having held it up for all to see, he thrust it into the air with astonishing velocity, and without so much as a visible tremor, zapped it in mid-air with a casual blast of its laser cannon.

'That could have been an incoming Soviet bomber, folks!' Marner said. 'Or an ICBM. Kids' play to our S.A.I.N.T. You move it on the ground, you sail it in the sea, you fly it in the air ... and S.A.I.N.T. can blast it to pieces.'

They were impressed. Senior military man spoke softly to senior military man, heads nodded, hands slipped quietly into pockets to find a pen to write down the name.

Thunder cracked ominously once more; this time it was close, and several people glanced up to see the source. An immense cumulo-nimbus had formed behind them, looming over the sprawling complex of the Nova laboratories.

'Maybe we'd better conclude our little presentation inside,' Marner said.

He nodded to Chigger, the young man in the suit, who throughout all this had been working hard and apparently unnoticed over his computer console. Chigger acknowledged the signal, pressed a key, and the little robot obediently rolled away.

As the crowd started to clamber down from the grandstand, one of the Generals moved quickly to Marner.

'I thought you said this was automatic, Marner.'

'So it is ... sir.' Marner's brow furrowed anxiously, but then with hyper control he worked it smooth again.

'What's with the kid at the console? Looked to me like he was controlling it.'

'Sir, I have to tell you. He was.' Marner looked relieved, and he began speaking glibly again. 'You see, we couldn't just turn one of these things *loose*. What you saw just now was not control ... but *restraint*. If we had put S.A.I.N.T. on full auto he would have wiped out everything in sight. Me, you, everyone here.'

The top soldier stared at him with steely eyes.

'Good one, Marner. I like it.' He slapped the President of the Nova Corporation on the shoulder, and marched off.

After checking quickly to see that Chigger and the other techs had everything under control, Marner set off in pursuit of his audience.

Thunder cracked again.

As they crossed the parking lot, Congresswoman Mills from Iowa fell into step beside him.

'Very impressive, Dr. Marner,' she said.

'Thank you, ma'am, thank you.' The congresswoman was on the House Defense Acquisitions Committee.

'You're a brilliant man.'

'Yes, I suppose –' Marner glanced anxiously at her. 'Ma'am, it's a *team* effort.'

'Of course.' She looked at a sheaf of notes she was carrying. 'The young man who designed S.A.I.N.T.? Weren't we supposed to be meeting him?'

'Yes, I've got an excellent team around me,' Marner said with complete modesty.

'Doctor ... Crosby?' she said.

'Ah! Dr. Crosby! Yes ... most unfortunate. Touch of 'flu. Has to stay inside at this time of year. The idiosyncrasies of genius, eh?'

'We're going to meet him?' she said.

'Brilliant man, brilliant. These are his babies, make no mistake.'

'I'd like to meet with him,' the congresswoman said again.

'And so you shall, ma'am, just as soon –'

To his transparent relief, the crowd had reached one of the security checkpoints, and in the scramble to find I.D. cards and passes, Marner managed to slip away from her.

Security was fierce ... that day. In fact, Nova Robotics had a well-established security team, under the strident command of E.G. Stonewall, formerly a colonel in the U.S. Marine Corps. Stonewall and his team – known throughout the company as his stormtroopers – actually did a pretty good job of protecting Nova Robotics from the rest of the world ... but these were modern times and while security was expensive, *visible* security made for good business. Just for the day, while the place was seething with top brass, the security team had been tripled in size by the adroit and timely acquisition of dozens of hired hands, all decked out in hastily purchased uniforms. To all intents and purposes Nova Robotics appeared to be swarming with paramilitary guards, but come sundown most of them would be back in the bars of nearby Pendleton.

Marner himself was briefly halted by one of the new boys, and had to search his pockets to find his I.D., cursing impatiently under his breath. When he was through the cordon, he set off at a brisk pace towards the R & D wing. After only a few yards he was relieved to see Chigger.

'All right,' he shouted. 'Where is he?'

'Crosby?'

'You know who I mean.'

'I guess he's back where he always is,' Chigger said. 'In the lab.'

'Then get him, and make it fast.'

'Dr. Marner, I've got to get the robots downloaded and

debriefed. It's going to rain, and there's a lot of expensive equip –'

'Chigger!'

'Very good, sahib.' Chigger waggled his head obediently, and moved off towards the lab. Because of his swarthy complexion he had fielded jokes about being a Pakistani all his life, and now whenever under stress he fell defensively into the role.

'And Chigger!'

He paused, looked back.

'I want Crosby in the conference room five minutes from *now*! You tell him if he stands me up this time he can get another job.'

'Okay.'

'This time I mean it.'

'Message received and understood.' Chigger waggled his head again, and hurried off ... but he'd heard Marner's threats before. They all had. The truth was that Crosby was irreplaceable and everyone, especially Marner, knew it.

There was a brilliant flash of lightning as he entered the lab, momentarily throwing bizarre shadows across the wall. Chigger glanced through the dust-lined window, saw the darkness of the sky, and hoped his tech team would get the robots back under cover before any damage was done.

Dr. Crosby – Newton Crosby Ph.D. – was absorbed in his work, as ever. Chigger had known him well for the five years they had worked together at Nova, and had rarely seen him less than totally wrapped up in his work. He had a power of concentration beyond anything Chigger had ever glimpsed; to his certain knowledge, Crosby had several times worked more than three days non-stop, without sleep or food, and only halting long enough to visit the john. The s.a.i.n.t. robots were *his*: he had dreamed them up, he had written the routines, tested and debugged them, developed the guidance systems, built the talk-back device, designed the weapons

11

system . . . if he'd been given half a chance he would not only have physically constructed the robots single-handed, he would personally have poured the duralumin into the casts.

Now he was hunched over his console in the familiar preoccupied way, jabbing expertly at two keyboards while watching the effect on a prosthetic hand he had assembled on the bench at his side.

'Hey, Crosby!' Chigger called.

No response. He hadn't expected one, but this time Crosby's ears were covered by headphones. Chigger lifted one of them up.

'Cros, come on! It started to rain, so they had to cut the demo short.'

Crosby's attention did not waver. Instead, he pressed a couple of keys, and on the bench the prosthetic hand raised a contemptuous finger in the general direction of Dr. Marner.

Thunder roared in the yard outside.

'Come on, Cros! You gotta go up there and hob-nob with the big boys.'

'Tell Marner that *this* is what I do. I'm not paid to hob-nob.'

Chigger reached over, and pulled out the jack-plug of the headphones. Crosby tore them off.

'Look, sahib,' Chigger said. '*I'm* not paid to be a messenger boy between you and Marner. Just this once, put on your tie?'

'Okay, you win.' Crosby opened a drawer in his desk and found the tie he kept there for funerals and Dr. Marner. 'What do they need me to tell them? That it costs eleven million dollars and kills people? I hate this PR crap. I ought to look for another job.' He stalked away.

'Everybody keeps telling me things I've heard a million times before,' Chigger said, but Crosby was already outside.

He followed him. The storm had broken, and as they sprinted across the yard the rain was coming down in sheets.

Chapter 3

Down in the Tech Zone, the basement of the building where the reception was taking place, the two chief technicians, Zack Wilhelm and Norman Aronsen, were down-loading the five assembled s.a.i.n.t. robots. All five had been brought in safely before the storm began.

Number One had been the performer on the battlefield, but the other four had been out there too, in a state of backup readiness. Since the in-house testing had been completed four weeks earlier, no more than trivial glitches had developed in any of the five, but with a major arms contract in the offing, and each unit on the card for eleven mil apiece, no one was taking any chances.

Debriefing was the relatively simple chore of hot-wiring each robot into the central databank, and creaming off its mass of stored information. In the process, all operations were recorded in a form that could be analysed at leisure, and it provided the not inconsiderable bonus that the robots were rendered harmless.

Everyone at Nova treated the s.a.i.n.t. robots with ungrudging respect. They were fascinating to work with, it was amusing to control them and make them perform tricks, their apparent intelligence – which was no more than an extensive vocabulary of behavioural responses programmed in by Crosby – continually astounded everyone on the staff . . . but they were *dangerous*.

Dr. Marner had not been prevaricating when he explained that the robot was under restraint. A single s.a.i.n.t. robot, running on full auto, was the meanest, most deadly weapon imaginable to man. It had sufficient inbuilt power to travel at high speed for more than a thousand miles. At the end of the journey it could muster enough destructive power to burn an entire city, neutralize fifty incoming nuclear warheads, destroy a battalion of tanks... and still have resources in reserve.

In the normal course of events, Chigger preferred to supervise the debriefing process himself, but Zack and Norman could be trusted and they had done the work dozens of times already. Nova had been in the robotics business a long time, and there were set procedures laid down. Every tech knew them backwards, and anyway they were *motivated*. They knew the routines had a purpose, and they weren't about to take shortcuts.

The first four robots had been safely disarmed and downloaded, and were waiting in a meek line for collection and transport to store. The last, Number Five, was just being hooked into the rig when something totally unprecedented happened.

Outside in the storm, on the edge of the complex, an electricity transformer took a full bolt of lightning. Two interrupts promptly fused, and at the speed of light a macrosurge of electricity entered the Tech Zone.

In short order (that is, within one-millionth of a millisecond), the following events took place:

Zack said, or started to say, 'Hey –'

A junction box exploded.

Fourteen separate computer slave units fused into irrecoverable lumps of molten silicon and plastic.

Every lightbulb in the basement went out.

Two power cables contorted into coils.

A shower of sparks gushed out of the air conditioning unit.

Norman was thrown to the ground.

The macrosurge entered the complex datastore of Number Five.

And Zack said, or finished saying, 'Hey –'

For an instant it seemed that Number Five had been kicked bodily from below. It leapt galvanically upwards, a web of static discharge snaked in brilliant blue lines all over it, its telescopic neck first contracted wildly then expanded at twice the speed, and as the robot clattered back to the floor the infra-red sensors behind its twin lens system glared brilliantly.

The binocular eyes were staring straight at Zack, and the mechanical shields above raised themselves like quizzical eyebrows.

'Judas H. *GOD!*' Zack said.

Behind him, from the floor, Norman said groggily, 'What in hell was *that?*'

'I don't know!'

Norman was getting painfully to his feet, shaking his head in a bleary way.

'What about Number Five?' he said.

Zack was staring transfixed into Number Five's eyes, where the unearthly red glow was beginning to dim.

'It took the full charge,' Zack said.

'Me too. Is it okay?'

'I think so.'

Very gingerly, Zack reached forward and prodded one of the buttons on the control panel situated on Number Five's chest. A relay inside clicked audibly.

'Thank God!' Zack said. 'It's our ass on the line if this thing got fried. Okay, good ... it's still functioning. So ...'

'So what?' Norman said, standing beside him. Neither he nor Zack had yet noticed that one of the side-effects of his own experience was that every hair on his head was now standing on end.

'So maybe,' Zack said slyly, 'maybe we didn't see anything ...'

'See what?' Norman said, getting the message.

'Shucks, I don't know. We were just here downloading like normal.' He turned to the line of robots. 'Okay, units! Command! Proceed to store.' In an undertone, he added, 'You buckets of crap ...'

Obediently, the five robots shuffled forward in the

direction of the loading bay, where the transport would pick them up. Five identical robots, meek and submissive, returning to safe-keeping.

But just as they moved through the doorway the last one, Number Five, swivelled his head slowly and glanced back. Later, thinking about it, Norman could have sworn it had a confused expression on its expressionless face ...

Chapter 4

Dr. Newton Crosby was wedged in a knot of people, his head bobbing from side to side like that of a spectator in the cheap seats at a tennis match. He was listening to the arms acquisition debate going to and fro.

He was actually more interested in watching the robots – however well he knew them, however familiar with them he became – he never tired of seeing the weird little things going about their pre-programmed tasks.

A week before, he and Chigger had taken an afternoon off and, more for the fun of it than anything else, had gotten hold of a few of the s.a.i.n.t. prototypes and programmed them to act as waiters. It had pleased Marner beyond belief at the time ... and carried away with the fun of it all, Chigger had driven into Pendleton and found some waitress uniforms somewhere.

Now the robots tooled backwards and forwards across the room, carrying trays of drinks and little dishes with snacks on them, moving with uncanny politeness towards each group of dignitaries and uttering their well-rehearsed lines.

'Let me offer you another drink, sir? Madam? I do recommend the salmon ... it was caught in a local stream. Have you tried one of these crackers? I'm sure you'll *love* them. No tip necessary, sir, but I do sincerely appreciate the gesture. No, sir, you may *not* see me afterwards! Have a nice day!'

And so on.

Just to hear it made Crosby want to howl with laughter, and run to the robots and hug them. And, judging by the level of happy excitement in the room, the guests were loving it all too. He even saw one of the secret service men, who earlier had been hovering around one of the Senators with a hand resting inside his jacket, chuck one of the robots under its 'chin,' and for a moment he looked almost human. The secret service man, that is.

But now Crosby was wedged in the heavy metal group, and no one was having fun. His head turned to and fro, to and fro.

'Eleven million dollars *each*, Dr. Marner?'

It was Congresswoman Mills, defending the interests of all the citizens of Iowa . . . and the House Committee too.

'That's the price, ma'am.'

'Have you any idea how much a nuclear warhead costs these days, Mr. Marner?'

'It's Doctor Marner –'

'Complete with delivery system?'

'Quite a few nickels, I'd say.'

'All up, armed, serviced and delivered, we're talking two million each. Less if it's multipled.'

'Multipled?'

'Multiple delivery. For that I can take out a city. And you want *eleven* for –?'

'Ma'am, we do package deals.'

To and fro, to and fro. Crosby was watching the beads of anxious sweat forming on Marner's temples.

At this point General Washburn, standing right next to Crosby, spoke up.

'Do you suppose the Soviets are on to this yet, Marner?' he said. Marner looked relieved.

'I'm glad you raised that point, General. Compared to conventional nuclear delivery systems, this is a *revolutionary* concept –'

'A *bizarre* concept,' said Congresswoman Mills.

'I'm with Dr. Marner on this. Give me a few of these babies, and I'll show you what I'd use them for.'

A waitress showed up.

'Hi, my name's Angie!' 'she' said, and giggled. 'I want you all to loosen up, and try one of my special cocktails.'

'Go away,' Dr. Marner said, who wanted to hear the rest of what the General had to say. But the robot had a spiel, and nothing short of being hot-wired into the database would stop it.

'... I want you all to have a real good time. Why don't you let me fix you a couple of my SuperNovas? They're the biggest bang in Oregon! Oh my, is that the time? Be seein' you later!'

She wheeled away. Crosby wanted to run after her, throw her to the ground and cuddle her.

'Go on, General,' said Marner.

'I see these things fitting into an all-out nuclear situation. High on primaries, low on collaterals. You see, if we could parachute a coupla dozen of these little guys behind the lines, let 'em hide out until the first strike blows over then ... blam! Each one carries a twenty megaton gift-wrapped goodie right up Main Street, Moscow!' His eyes were looking misty. 'We'd call it, call it... Operation Gotcha Last!'

There was an immense flash outside, followed at once by a mighty *crack!* of thunder ... and the lights briefly went out. They came on again so quickly no one except Marner, Crosby and Chigger even noticed ... and yet at that very moment, down in the basement, Zack and Norman were having a bad time.

Dr. Marner said, without a trace of worry, 'Quite so, General. I can see you appreciate all the potential of the S.A.I.N.T. robots.'

'I like to think so, Marner.'

'Dr. Crosby's design is, of course, *multi*-functional. Isn't that so, Newton?'

Crosby realized he was still enmeshed in the sales pitch. He blinked.

Marner went on, 'We all like to think of S.A.I.N.T. as a cross between a computer and a guerrilla bandit. Give the Third World what they've been giving us. These things can do their own maintenance, Congresswoman! Even rebuild their own components if they're damaged! They'll function for years, if necessary. And, all the while, remain capable of all manner of offensive and defensive manoeuvres.'

Crosby, keen to enter the conversation since he had at long last been addressed, cleared his throat.

'Of course,' he said earnestly. 'It'd be just wonderful for all sorts of *non*-military uses. You know, my original designs were simply intended –' An elbow went into his ribs.

Marner said, 'Absolutely! Plenty of different applications ... but not while we have to classify it as a top secret weapon, that's right, isn't it Crosby?' He glanced quickly over his shoulder as if someone had just called his name. 'Excuse me, General, Congresswoman? We do have to make an effort to say hello to everybody ...' He propelled Crosby away from the group.

'Did I say something wrong, Dr. Marner?'

'Keep smiling, and leave the clever stuff to me. Okay?'

'Sure, I don't mind. I think I'll get a drink.'

Marner walked towards another close-knit group, an oily smile spreading across his insipid face.

Crosby saw one of the waitresses, and neatly intercepted her.

'Well, hi there, handsome! You can call me Lois, and I know you and I are going to be real good friends –' Crosby cut off the flow by jabbing expertly at one of the buttons on the front of the machine, then could not help looking round guiltily, as if he had impulsively stuck his hand down the front of a woman's dress. With the robot waitress temporarily immobilized, Crosby took one of the glasses and poured into it the contents of three others. He gave the robot another furtive press on its chest, then hurried away before it could start in on him again.

Marner, meanwhile, was embroiled with the Senator, feeling uncomfortable with the secret service men standing there in their dark glasses and pretending not to listen. They kept staring around the room in a way that made Marner think they were noticing something. He kept wanting to look around and see what was going on.

'No, Senator,' he was saying. 'Nowhere *near* that amount. We're talking developmental bucks at the moment. By the time we're tooled up and in production I expect the cost per unit could come down as low as three, maybe three and a half million. Of course, we'd be skinned at that price. Wouldn't make a dime on them.'

'You know what a nuclear warhead costs, Marner?'

'Yeah, but you can't use it twice.' Marner had had time to think about that one. It was his only real triumph that day.

Even so, he was making heavy weather of it all, and was greatly relieved when a low, familiar rumbling noise sounded in the corridor outside.

The doors opened, and with a certain bravura the S.A.I.N.T. robots wheeled into the room, gleaming wonderfully.

'Excuse me!' Marner said. He clapped his hands to draw attention to himself, and said in a loud voice, 'Ladies and gentlemen! Our stars are here!'

But even as he spoke he was wishing he had not been quite so hasty. It did not take him long to notice - indeed, he did not even need every finger on his hand to work it out - that one of the robots was missing. Spotting Chigger standing by the door, he hurried over, passing the robots on the way. He registered each one's number as he passed.

'What's wrong, Chigger?' he said. 'Where's Number Five?'

'I've just been trying to find out.'

'Well...?'

'We ... don't exactly know. That is ... exactly.'

'Try being a bit more specific.'

'According to Zack it left the debriefing station, and all was well. But somewhere along the way it just... disappeared.'

In the background, the newly arrived robots were the centre of attention. People were looking expectantly in Marner's direction.

'I've got to get on with this,' Marner said. His face worked with anxiety, then a deadly calm seemed to come over him. His next words sent a chill to Chigger's heart.

'Get Stonewall on to this,' he said.

Chapter 5

After leaving the debriefing station the five S.A.I.N.T. robots propelled themselves obediently down the corridor. The crisp formation, precise and regulated, was heading for the reception upstairs. As planned, Number One went first, followed in numerical order by all the others.

They trundled along, deadly, purposeful and full of menace. Four pairs of mechanical eyes stared straight ahead, like those of well-drilled soldiers.

But bringing up the rear was Number Five, and although he maintained the pace with all the others, *his* eyes were not stolidly forward-looking.

Instead, he craned his neck from side to side, his eyes opened wide, his metal eyeshades raised high. The voice simulator outlet – a modular grille – hung open in wonder.

Halfway to the iron staircase – a little thing like a flight of steps was no hindrance to a S.A.I.N.T. – one of Crosby's waitresses passed in the other direction, 'her' tray of drinks now empty.

As she went by, she was muttering sexily to herself, '... I guess that's okay. You can call me, if you like. Just ask for Laura-Lee. See you later, big boy...'

Number Five seemed to trip, and fell out of step at once.

He wheeled around, and hurried after her.

Her comms cable was trailing behind her, snaking in a most alluring way.

Number Five zigzagged after it, his lenses gleaming.

Not looking where he was going, Number Five missed the sharp turn into the service area, and as the waitress did a sharp right, he lurched straight onwards, his face turned towards her.

With a clatter like an enamel bucket falling on concrete, he bashed into a wall.

He recoiled, shook his head . . . and for a moment seemed unclear of where he was. His head rotated through three hundred and sixty degrees, then his eyes fixed on a light switch, fixed to the wall by the entrance to the service area.

He moved to it, extended an arm, then flicked the switch off and on with great interest. The causal connection between this action and the light turning on and off immediately dawned on him, and he began moving the switch with increasing speed.

After a few seconds of this, the lightbulb exploded and fine glass tinkled down.

Number Five reached up a second arm, and jabbed his finger into the remains of the bulb. A bolt of electricity coursed through him. Deep inside his chest, relays whirred in protest.

To Number Five it was like a quickening of the heart.

He remembered the sexy waitress and, tiring of the light socket, he wheeled into the service area in belated pursuit of her.

Luck was against him. No sooner had he passed through the door than another robot – menial, brainless thing – came unexpectedly from the side pushing an immense garbage can . . . and Number Five was scooped along in front of it.

Number Five squawked his protest, but the kitchen robot was of the lowest order . . . had he even understood, it would have taken him at least twenty milliseconds to respond. Too late!

Number Five and all the rubbish were propelled ignominiously into the garbage chute. Making undignified clanking noises, Number Five slid down and down, arms and caterpillar treads akimbo. Empty paper cups, plastic knives and masses and masses of uneaten food skittered around him.

The ordeal came to an end with a loud thudding noise, and a torrent of messy garbage. Number Five had landed head first, and could only wait patiently while the sickly stuff slithered and squashed around him.

A minute passed in silence.

Then Number Five's periscope prodded experimentally towards the light. It rotated once, took in the view, and retracted.

Number Five emerged, shedding fragments of smoked salmon, liver paste, walnut salad and potato chips.

He was in the Nova complex's refuse tip, and to him it seemed beautiful beyond belief. He squeaked in pleasure, and accelerated to full speed, dashing around the squalid yard, his caterpillar treads throwing up a spray of pulverized rubbish. The sun shone down as the storm cloud cleared away, and its rays warmed his metal skin.

Encouraged by this, Number Five saw the gate that led out of the yard and sped through it. Freedom loomed.

He went as fast as his on-board motor would propel him, taking a straight line ... anywhere that was away from Nova!

Then freedom was denied him. His sensors picked up the chain-link fence before his lenses could actually see it, and he slowed in time to stop himself hurtling straight into it.

He paused, and regarded the obstacle with professional interest. Such a barrier was as great a problem to him as a spider's web was to a bullet, but in his new dawning awareness, Number Five suspected, were he to push his way through, that it might somehow signal his location to those who wished to know it. Caution welled up in him, so he rolled along parallel to it, letting one of his metal fingers run along the gaps in the fence.

Clink, clink, clink, it went, bringing joy to Number Five's soul.

'CLINK!' he said ... then, after much thought, 'CLINK CLINK, *CLINK*!'

He became completely wrapped up in this game, and did not notice that the ground on which he was travelling had suddenly acquired a steep gradient.

He wheeled up this, then clattered to a halt in confusion. Number Five was surrounded by steel drums. He started in surprise, and then again in interest. He began to peer in a fascinated way at the one closest to him.

He was receptive to everything; all that he saw was of equal interest.

But the fascination soon died when he realized that the steel drum, compared with, say, even the kitchen robot, was as near brainless as it was possible to be.

'Null intelligence!' he said dismissively, and turned to the next, eternally optimistic.

This one was different. It had no brain – this he established at once – but perched on its lid was a butterfly. It had broad wings, half poised for flight, coloured deep brown with startling orange patches.

Number Five turned up his visual receptors full, and moved his head gently forward. He transmitted all the usual coded signals of identification, challenge and response ... but the butterfly paid him no attention.

This careless disregard fascinated Number Five even more. It was so ... so ... so ...

He possessed no word for it in his limited vocabulary.

But it made him feel clumsy and big, and he moved back. He looked down at himself, and discovered that in his haste to get away from the buildings he was still covered in bits of the garbage.

No wonder the butterfly would not speak to him!

He rolled back a few inches, then quickly ionized his outer shell. All the bits of rubbish sprang away from him in a spherical cloud. Around him, the empty steel drums all thudded into each other as they were briefly magnetized ...

But at least he was clean, and Number Five went in search of the butterfly again. Something must have disturbed it – perhaps his dramatic cleansing operation had made it fly away – because he could find it no more.

He had little time to reflect on this, because a new distraction appeared. A human was passing close by!

Number Five ducked down, and watched through his periscope.

The man went past the drums, only his head in view, and with much noise pushed up the ramp that Number Five had climbed when he was distracted by the fence.

Suddenly, Number Five realized that in his pre-occupations he had strayed on to the back of a truck. He retracted his periscope, and waited patiently while the man went back to his cab, started the engine and drove slowly away.

When they were under way, Number Five raised his head for a better view . . . then pulled down again when he saw that the truck was approaching the main gate! The truck halted, and the relays in Number Five's chest beat a little more quickly.

Another human said, 'Sign this, Jake.'

A pause.

Then, 'I'll be back in a while.'

'Okay, okay. You on for a game of cards tonight?'

'You bet.'

'Okay . . . see ya later.'

The engine started up again, and the truck moved forward. When it had gone some way, Number Five raised his periscope and looked back at the gate. The red and white striped bar at the gate was being lowered.

The steel drums rocked and clanged around him. The warm sun beat down on him. The wind blew over his antennae.

He was free!

Chapter 6

Colonel E.G. Stonewall was feeling happy and fulfilled. Indeed, he was practically bursting with pleasure and pride. Two years of pent-up energy all to be released by a flash of lightning!

At last he had something to which he could turn his unique talents.

E.G. was known by various names and in various ways, depending on which level of the corporation you were listening in on. The intellectuals up in the Artificial Intelligence lab called him 'For Example,' this being some kind of meaningful joke at the expense of his initials that no one else ever laughed at. Dr. Marner sometimes called him 'E.G.', sometimes 'Colonel Stonewall', and, when tired and distracted, sometimes 'sir'. All of these were to E.G.'s liking.

His security troops called him 'Edward G.,' which was less to his liking, but made his chest puff up a bit. They also called him 'sir' (to his face), and 'asshole' (when they were a minimum of twenty miles from him). Chigger called him 'Bimbo,' but then he called everyone that from time to time and, when confronted with the actual presence of E.G., called him nothing at all.

Crosby would have liked to maintain Chigger's air of supreme indifference, but then Chigger had a reputation for Eastern transcendentalism (based more on the way he looked than on the way he acted), and Crosby was highly responsive to what he interpreted as threats.

E.G. Stonewall threatened everything that Crosby stood for. He threatened him physically (Crosby knew as a matter of indisputable fact that Stonewall could break him in half with one hand), intellectually (in Stonewall's version of the universe anyone who could think was an enemy) and ideologically (Stonewall summed up, for Crosby, everything that was making America bad, from his love of mindless violence, through his rabid right-wing politics to his instinctive aggression, need for revenge, distrust of strangers, hatred of socialism, ignorance of the world ... and so on into the pit of anarchy that awaited, in a just society, those of his ilk).

If Crosby had a name for Stonewall it was probably unutterable, and certainly unprintable ... and rather than provoke a fight he would lose in the first second, Crosby had chosen to pretend that Stonewall did not exist.

Stonewall also summed up his peculiar dilemma about Nova Robotics.

Crosby knew there was probably no other corporation, agency or organization he could work for who would give him such freedom to develop and experiment with robots. By his achievements, he had reached a point where he could demand, and expect, the corporation to provide him with any facility he needed ... however bizarre or expensive it might be. They trusted him, because he had always come up with what they wanted.

And that, paradoxically, was the problem. What they wanted was an eleven-million dollar killing machine. They had it now, and it worked. But what Crosby had intended all along was the finest, highest form of artificial intelligence, the machine that had soul, the robot that thought for itself.

Without Nova he could never have done it. With Nova he had done it and regretted that he had done it.

E.G. Stonewall hated intelligence, hated life. He was a man who would kill in case he himself was killed (and call it pre-emptive self-defence), and so long as Nova Robotics produced machines that were, so to speak, on his side, he remained unaroused, unprovoked.

But Number Five had fled the coop, and had become another enemy.

Stonewall himself would have been incapable of such

reasoned thinking, however unpleasant. He was in his own way a robot, a man whose intelligence was artificially lowered by the closed state of his mind.

All he knew, when he got the word from Marner, was that at last his hour had come. Those years of frustrating practice, of sending out patrols of the outer fence of the complex, of drilling his troops with the ever-present need for alertness, of maintaining a state of readiness . . . all had come to pass.

He was ready . . . God, he was ready!

'Got anything yet, Colonel Stonewall?' said Marner.

'I got a dozen troops on the perimeter. I got another ten or so scouring the grounds. We got video scan of the whole range.'

'Have you found the robot?'

'Not yet, sir. Leave it to me.'

He raised a microphone to his mouth and barked a series of commands into it. Marner winced away, but then the urgency of the moment impelled him back again.

A distorted voice came through the static, and Stonewall responded. He jabbed at a slide control, and the picture on one of the overhead monitors zoomed with a sickening motion, went out of focus, sharpened up, then drifted out of focus again.

'We got it, we got the little son of a –' Stonewall checked himself. 'I mean, Dr. Marner, we found your robot for you. B Squad is moving in right now.'

Another monitor showed a fleeting glimpse of a group of uniformed men, rifles unslung, galloping ferociously across a patch of grass.

'I don't see it,' Marner said.

'There! There!'

Stonewall jerked a thumb at the first monitor, where, in the blurry mists of bad photography, a small shiny object could be just about discerned. Marner reached over to tighten the focus, but his hand was slapped down by Stonewall.

'Leave it to me!' he shouted in excitement, then added, 'Sir.' While yelling more incoherent orders into the microphone, Stonewall made jerky adjustments to the monitor's controls, and at last a kind of focus was achieved.

Dr. Marner squinted at the picture.

'Colonel Stonewall . . . that looks rather like a fire hydrant to me.'

'Leave it to the professionals, sir.' Stonewall resumed his bawling noise.

'It's painted *red*!' Marner said, his voice high-pitched with frustration.

'It is?'

'Number Five is silver coloured. Not red.'

At last Stonewall condescended to look at the picture.

When he started yelling into the microphone again, he was screaming abuse at B Squad.

'What about the perimeter gates?' Marner said. 'Are they all sealed off?'

'We did it straight away, sir.'

'What about the main gate?' Marner pointed at the monitor screen right at the end of the row. This showed a steady picture, in perfect focus, of an open main gate, a guard walking slowly back into his hut . . . and a truck moving into the distance trailing a thin cloud of exhaust smoke.

The back of Stonewall's neck started to go red under his short grey hair.

Chigger, who had been standing in the quiet area at the back of the operations room, decided he had seen enough.

He moved away softly, then walked quickly up to the main block, where the reception was still in progress.

He found Crosby at once, standing inconspicuously at the side, leaning casually against a wall and nursing a small glass.

'You'd better come, Bimbo,' Chigger said.

'I'm concentrating on getting drunk.'

'Number Five's got away.'

31

Crosby appeared to smile, but he kept his face straight.

'Number Five's a big boy. He can look after himself. I'll call him up on the link, bring him in.'

'Stonewall's out to get him.'

'You're kidding!'

'I kid you not, Bimbo. He's got the goons out there, and they're going to shoot to kill.'

In one swift movement, Crosby put down his glass and levered himself away from the wall.

Once he and Chigger were away from the guests they began to run.

As they entered the operations room, Stonewall was still bawling incomprehensibly into his microphone, while several nervous technicians were standing in a semi-circle behind him. Dr. Marner had apparently given up any hope of a meaningful dialogue with the security chief, and had moved to the master control chair. This was always Crosby's place, where all the testing and evaluation of the robots had been carried out.

Marner saw him come in, and moved gratefully out of the chair.

'Where the hell have you been?' he said.

'Hob-nobbing ... just like you told me.'

'Look, Crosby ... get Number Five back. Stonewall's going crazy.'

'Leave it to me, sir.'

Crosby slipped naturally into the seat, and pulled the moveable console towards him. His fingers raced across the keys, entering the series of commands that logged him on as controller. Marner watched with some respect.

'Okay, sir ... let's get this going,' Crosby said. 'You tried the return code, of course?'

'Yes ... nothing. And I put out the abort command, the halt command, and all the standard idents.'

'What about the operational cancel?'

'I was just getting to that.'

32

'Okay...'

Crosby's concentration turned fully on the problem in hand. He coded in the operational cancel, confirmed it, repeated it, and sent it. He waited ... but the green monitor screen remained blank.

'Hmm,' he said, almost to himself. 'No response.'

'So...?' Marner said.

'Are you sure Number Five's operational? He doesn't seem to be on-line.'

'He's out there somewhere.'

'But is he working normally?'

'Crosby, he's *escaped*! He's not normal.'

'Okaaay... I'll try the emergency override.'

He fished in his pocket for a key, slipped it into a lock on the side of the console, and used the keys to toggle the signal, confirming that the override was working. Then he typed: **REPORT YOUR POSITION.**

The cursor blinked on and off, then moved with a crazy motion to the middle of the screen. Crosby's message disappeared, to be replaced by: **MALFUNCTION. NEED INPUT.**

Marner said, 'What the hell does that mean?'

'It means a lot of things. He's out there, he's operational ... and he's responding. But –'

'But what?'

Crosby was shaking his head slowly, beginning to appreciate the size of the problem.

'At the bottom line it means he's forgotten how to triangulate his position. That's okay ... we got lots of ways of locking in on him. But if he can't triangulate, then we can't instruct him, which means we can't tell him where to go ... which means –'

'– He's out of control,' Chigger said.

'In a sense, yes,' Crosby said, still intrigued by the intellectual nature of the problem.

'For God's sake, Crosby!' Marner said.

Crosby typed in at the keyboard: **FOLLOW HOMING SIGNAL**.

Quick as a flash, the answer came back: **NEGATIVE. ENGAGED**.

Not content with this, the screen started to scroll repetitions:

ENGAGED.

       ENGAGED.

              ENGAGED.

                     ENGAGED.

Crosby rubbed his hands together. 'Engaged, Number Five?' he said out loud. 'Engaged in what?'

'This isn't funny,' Marner said.

'No, but it's damned interesting. You see, when he's "engaged" it means he's running diagnostics, testing his logic circuits. That's a *prima facie* acceptance by the central processing unit that something's wrong. Number Five's in trouble, he doesn't *know* he's in trouble, and yet he's acting as if he's *in* trouble... so he keeps running diagnostics. Fascinating!'

'Cros, they keep checking out,' Chigger said. 'He wouldn't keep repeating if there was something wrong. We get closedown when there is.'

Crosby stared thoughtfully at the monitor, where the word **ENGAGED** kept scrolling down.

'I guess you're right,' he said. 'I'll just shut him down, then we can go out and pick him up.'

He typed a new comand: **INTERRUPT PRIMARY POWER**.

Without even a pause, the answer came back: **UNABLE. MALFUNCTION**.

'So what does *that* mean?' Marner said.

'It means... we've got one very screwed-up robot out there.'

'What's the matter with it? Is it having a nervous breakdown? Is it angry? What?'

Crosby looked up at his boss with a serious face.

'It's a machine, Dr. Marner,' he said. 'It doesn't get angry. It doesn't get happy. It doesn't laugh at your jokes. It –'

And Chigger joined in the familiar litany: '– *it just runs programs.*'

They glanced at each other.

'It *usually* runs programs,' Chigger said.

'Listen, Chigger,' Crosby said. 'Did Number Five go out with a finder beacon?'

'Yeah . . . he's supposed to have one.'

'Okay. I should at least be able to turn that on.' He pressed a new sequence of keys.

'Bingo!' he said.

The screen output changed dramatically. A schematic diagram of the whole complex appeared. Crosby touched a key, and it was promptly echoed to the master monitor close to where Stonewall was still standing. As if seen from a moving point somewhere above, the diagram wheeled and went into perspective, and the image enlarged to take in the surrounding country. A red illuminated blip came into view, flashing on and off.

Crosby did a double-take. Marner looked shocked.

'Jesus Christ!' he said. 'Crosby, is this thing right? The robot's outside the compound perimeter!'

'That's what it looks like to me,' Crosby said.

'Oh, my God,' Chigger said. 'It's armed to the hilt.'

'What?' Crosby said.

Marner went one better.

'*WHAT*?' he shouted.

'It hadn't been disarmed when it broke away,' Chigger said, as calmly as possible. 'It's fully functional.'

Marner backed away, found a chair. He sank into it wearily. 'Crosby . . . what's it going to *do*?'

'That's hard to say,' Crosby replied, very seriously. 'I mean, it's malfunctioning. Maybe it won't do anything.' He shrugged. 'But then, maybe . . .'

35

'It could decide to blow away anything that moves!' Marner said.

'Depends what it is,' Crosby said, defending his pride and joy.

'Depends what it *thinks* it is,' Chigger said, and turned away to stare through the window, out to the bare compound and beyond to the undulating, peaceful countryside.

Chapter 7

Number Five enjoyed the motion of the truck, lurching to and fro on the dusty road. He had discovered that the back of the driver's head could be seen through a glass panel in the cab, and that the driver's face could be seen reflected in the mirror, so he kept his head down and did not try to extend his periscope.

To while away the time he sent out receptor vectors to the truck's engine, and analysed the electrical noise it emitted.

When he had worked out the language the truck spoke, Number Five ventured a message of greetings.

Roughly translated, it came out as, 'Brrrrm...'

For some reason the truck did not reply, so Number Five sat silently and waited for the ride to end.

The journey was not a long one. About one mile, six hundred and seventy-two yards, one foot and seven point three six one inches from the main gate (by Number Five's rough estimate) the truck turned off the road into an area of flattened ground where hundreds of steel drums were stored. As the truck braked to a noisy halt, Number Five did not wait for the driver to open the tailgate, but leapt over the side and scorched back towards the road. He moved so quickly that his new escape was shrouded by the cloud of dust thrown up by the truck as it had turned.

He was soon rolling along peacefully through trees, his visual receptors turned up full, his head turning from side to side with an efficient sweeping motion.

Everything he saw went into his database; everything in his database added to the sum of his knowledge.

As knowledge grew in him, the immense timelessness of the forest seeped into his soul. He was affected by the static grandeur of the trees, the stillness of the air, the quietude of the soil and the cover of fallen leaves.

Gradually Number Five's frantic need to escape leeched away from him, and he began to slow.

As the peaceful forest filled his input banks, he came to a halt. He stood motionless for several minutes, staring at the ground, absent-mindedly running a few chemical analyses of the soil... but to all intents and purposes at ease and in harmony with nature.

Something landed on his head, causing him to start mentally. With great care he extended his periscope, then canted it around to see.

A squirrel was sitting on his head, holding the husk of a nut in its little paws and chewing vigorously. Flakes of the husk drifted down.

Number Five watched with great interest.

A moment later, a bird fluttered down from a tree and landed on one of his arms.

Keeping very still, Number Five sent out a recognition signal. To his immense satisfaction, the bird responded.

'Cheep!' it said.

Happiness rose in Number Five. Full of enthusiasm he returned the signal.

'*Cheep!*' he cried at maximum volume. '*Cheep, cheep, CHEEP!*' Then, for good measure, he added, '*Clink, clink, CLINK!*'

The squirrel scuttled away; the bird was gone.

Number Five set out in search of them, emitting melancholy 'cheep' and 'clink' noises... and, when these did not succeed, an occasional 'brrrrm'.

His search brought him back to the edge of the road, and because it looked as if it might lead somewhere interesting he set off along it, going slowly in case he saw any more animals, but definitely heading *somewhere*.

Then he saw his first advertising billboard.

Chapter 8

Marner was pacing impatiently in the operations room, trying not to watch the flashing blip on the display. Crosby was hunched over the keyboard, Chigger standing behind him.

'It's *moving* again, Crosby!'

'Yes, but I'm monitoring him all the way.'

'I don't want you to monitor it . . . I want you to pull it back in!'

'I'm working on it, Dr. Marner. I'm working on it.'

Something seemed to snap in the older man.

'That does it!' he said. 'I'm going to send Stonewall out to eliminate it.'

A low feeling hit Crosby. Stonewall had left the operations room some minutes before, bringing a sense of relief to all those present. It had seemed then that Stonewall was off the case.

'Are you serious?' Crosby said. 'He'll destroy it.'

'That's the idea, yes.'

'But how am I going to study the problem?'

'The problem, Dr. Crosby, is that Number Five is malfunctioning.'

'Sure he is . . . but this kind of malfunction is extremely valuable. We should at least make every effort to bring him back intact before turning Stonewall loose on him.'

'And what if we *can't* bring him back?' Marner said. 'If that unit goes out and melts down a busload of nuns, are you going to write the press release?'

Crosby shrugged his despair.

'Okay, okay,' he said. 'But let's think before we panic.'

'While you're thinking, Number Five's out there getting ready to melt something down.'

Desperately, Crosby said, 'Look, Dr. Marner. We know exactly where he is. He's rolling along slowly, shows no sign of speeding up. Even if he did, even if he hit top speed . . . he isn't going to reach anywhere populated for at least twenty minutes. Okay?'

Chigger threw in his support. 'Eleven million dollars, Dr. Marner . . .'

'I'm acutely aware of that.' Dr. Marner ran his fingers through his thinning hair. 'All right, you've got twenty minutes.'

Crosby and Chigger exchanged a look of relief, and Crosby turned back to the keyboard. A new idea had occurred to him, a way of getting Number Five perhaps to switch himself off manually.

At the main display, Dr. Marner picked up a phone.

'Find me Colonel Stonewall,' he said, distinctly. Chigger and Crosby stared at him in disbelief. 'Stonewall?' Marner said. 'I want you to get your emergency team together.'

The earpiece made a squawking sound, and Marner winced.

'Yes, E.G., now. Get out there, find the unit and contain it. We've still got time to avoid an incident.'

As the earpiece squawked again, Crosby rose half out of his seat.

'Hey, Dr. Marner! Don't send those apes out yet! Give me a chance, okay?'

Covering the mouthpiece with his hand, Marner turned to face him.

'You've got your twenty minutes,' he said nastily. 'I want Stonewall out there as backup.'

Crosby dived across the room, and before Marner could resist he had snatched the telephone receiver from him.

'Stonewall?' Crosby shouted. 'This is Crosby.' Offensive noises blared from the earpiece, so Crosby changed tack. 'Discretion,' he said in a more reasonable voice. 'You understand? Use some discretion. Just try to capture the unit. We've got to examine Number Five undamaged.'

The phone howled as it was disconnected at the other end.

Crosby suppressed his irritation, shouldered his way past Marner, and returned to his keyboard.

The phone rang again, and Marner snatched it up.

'Yes?' he said. 'What? No... tell them I've got food poisoning. I can't get back there right now.' He slammed down the phone.

Chigger said quietly to Crosby, 'I've had an idea. What about using scramble sequence?'

'What about it?' Crosby's mind was still distracted by the recent memory of Stonewall's voice.

'He's not responding to plain language. Maybe he'll still read code.'

Crosby clicked finger and thumb together.

'Right! Let's try it!'

'I set up the decoder.'

'Okaaay... let's scramble one.' Crosby was back in his element; intelligence against artificial intelligence.

His fingers dashed expertly over the keys. The coded sequences for scrambling commands had not yet been fully debugged, but they worked most of the time. The need for them hadn't so far arisen... the team had been postponing the work until a firm military contract was in hand. Code was the sort of detail that had to come later.

Even so, there were six separate levels of codable memory in Number Five, and he was known to react to all of them.

Having set up the code matrix, Crosby transmitted the first block.

Instantly, Number Five responded. A familiar pattern of hex arithmetic formed on the screen.

'It's working!' Chigger said.

'I'm glad you two are enjoying this so much.' It was Marner, a sardonic scowl on his face.

Crosby ignored him. He typed at the keyboard: **RETURN TO D-STATION**.

Hex arithmetic sorted itself efficiently across the display. Then the scrambling cleared, and Number Five's answer came back to the screen: **IT'S THE REAL THING!**

'*What?*' said Chigger.

'Damned if I know,' Crosby said.

'I'm gonna have a Coke,' Chigger said, and walked away, humming the jingle to himself.

Chapter 9

'It's the real thing!'

Number Five spoke the words haltingly, as his optical character scanner deciphered the words from the fading red and white billboard. The upper and lower valves of his vocal simulator slapped to and fro as the subliminal images of thirst, ice-cold fizzy drinks, sharp carbonated bubbles, etc., came swimming out of the advertisement's design.

Staring up at it, Number Five said, 'Need input. Need input. Need the real thing!'

He backed away, and propelled himself further along.

The billboard had been posted above a gas station, abandoned long ago. Heaps of unidentifiable bits of broken machinery were scattered around, dark red with rust. They saddened Number Five.

Out front, on a forecourt where scrubby grass now grew, a solitary gas pump stood neglected. Number Five went across to it, ran a recognition scan, and realized at once that it too was dead.

'Need input,' he said, more from necessity than hope. He saw that it had a long rubber tube attached to a crude kind of tap, so he pulled this down and peered into the nozzle with one lens. He could see nothing, but his olfactory receptors detected the residue of petrochemical substances.

'Not real thing!' he said. 'Need input.'

The pump had a dial set to zero. Number Five ran an interrupt sequence across it, and the hands obligingly rotated once around the dial. Again Number Five sniffed at the nozzle, but no gasoline had appeared.

Feeling sorry for the dead machine, Number Five backed away to think things over.

He rolled out into the middle of the road, and hunched

himself down inconspicuously. In this position he was capable of vast computing energy, and it was time he explored every last byte in his memory store to see if there were any data there he could input for himself.

It was while he was still crouching in this place, a few minutes later, that events began to move very fast indeed.

Chapter 10

E.G. Stonewall was in his jeep when the call from Dr. Marner came through on the field telephone. Stonewall and the rest of his emergency team were bouncing along the country roads in pleasurable pursuit of the missing robot, when Marner authorized him to start doing exactly that.

Stonewall's lip curled contemptuously, and he pretended he'd get going ... but then Crosby came on the line.

'Oh yes, sir, Mister Crosby,' Stonewall yelled. 'We'll make every effort to take the little bastard alive!'

He hung up violently, took the stub of his cigar from his mouth and spat a stream of yellow saliva over the side. Then he reached behind him, and brought out his м-16 rifle. He rattled the auto-loading mechanism.

'My sweet ass!' he said, to no one in particular, but presumably to his driver, who was the only person within earshot. 'This is what I've been waiting for! A chance to go up against one of those cans of garbage. Ain't no robot ever gonna outsmart your well-trained foot soldier! And that wimp wants me to take it alive!'

He butted the driver with the heel of his hand.

'Speed up, soldier!'

'Yes, sir.'

Stonewall preened himself, and surveyed the surrounding land. Then he raised the field telephone again.

'All units!' he barked. 'Check in!'

He had to repeat the order twice, but in the end all his men had acknowledged his signal. On the computerized board in front of him – which, incidentally, had been designed and built by Crosby – a neat row of eight red lights gleamed obediently, telling Stonewall that all units could hear him.

'It's shoot-to-kill time, men. That little heap of scrap is the deadliest crittur this side of the Iron Curtain. It's him or it's you. Go for it, shoot on sight! Speed up, and let's get the war over! Remember . . . if you don't get *it*, it will get *you*!'

One of the units represented by a little red light on Stonewall's computerized board was a rental truck, being driven by two hired temporary security men. They were called Duke and Otis.

When not being a temporary security man for Nova Robotics, Duke worked behind a bar in Pendleton. Otis, when not ditto, spent a lot of time in the same bar, buying drinks from Duke.

They had taken the day's job because it had seemed to be a quick two hundred bucks each for having to do not very much.

Duke, who was driving, glanced at Otis. Otis, who had taken the call from Stonewall, hung the transceiver back on its hook.

'Y'hear that, Duke?' he said.

'Sure did.'

'Better speed up, so we can shoot on sight.'

'Sure will.'

Duke slowed down.

Meanwhile, Number Five was still having a think, huddled up in the centre of the road.

'Does that gadget work?' Duke said.

Otis, who had been trying to figure it out, cuffed it with the side of his hand. Nothing much seemed to change.

'The Colonel said it was some kind of tracer. He said it would show a flashing orange light when we got close enough.'

'Is it flashing?'

'Ain't doing a thing.'

'Good.'

Duke continued his leisurely drive through the piney woods. He kept glancing nervously at the tracer, just in case it started flashing.

'You know, Otis,' he said. 'You know what's gonna happen? If that little robot thinks we're a Russian tank, it's barbecue time and we're the weenies.'

'That serious, huh?'

'You heard the man. It's him or us. What say we blow him away on sight?'

'Think we should?'

'I dunno. What about you?'

'Did I say different?' Otis exclaimed. 'I know what I ain't gonna do, and that's try to take his ass alive. You saw what it did to those tanks. And this one's gone crazy!'

Duke drove on in silence.

'I say we blow him away,' he said at last. 'But before we do that, why don't we just make sure we don't find him?'

He eased his foot from the accelerator pedal, and the truck slowed down from its sluggish ten miles an hour to an almost stationary five miles an hour.

Stonewall called in, and with something of a gulp Otis confirmed that they were screaming about the countryside in hot pursuit.

As he hung the transceiver back on the hook, something orange flashed brightly on the screen of the tracer.

'Oh, my God!' Otis shouted. 'Look at that!'

Duke peered over to see.

'What say we turn that gismo off?' he said.

'Can't be done,' said Otis. 'I already tried.'

The flashing got brighter, and Otis pressed back from it into his seat.

'Holy shit!' he cried. 'He's got us! He's got us!'

Duke was looking out of the cab windows from side to side. 'I can't see him!'

'We're right on top of him!'

The flashing had steadied now into a continuous glare of orange light.

Meanwhile, Number Five was still having a think, huddled up in the centre of the road. He did not see the truck racing towards him, at its almost stationary speed of five miles an hour . . .

When a loud *clang*! came from the front of the truck, Duke almost died of fright, and Otis screamed and made a frantic backwards scrambling motion.

'Slow down, slow down!' Otis yelled.

Duke responded by flattening his foot against the gas pedal, and the truck began to accelerate.

The orange light on the tracer glared at them.

Otis lunged at the transceiver, and held down the call button.

Stonewall came on.

'What?' he snapped.

'Captain, sir . . . I mean Colonel! He's got us! I mean, we found him!'

'Where are you?'

Otis covered the microphone with his hand.

'Where are we, Duke?'

'Getting the hell out of here.' The truck was going a healthy fifty-five now, and still accelerating . . . but the orange tracer was just as steady, just as bright.

'We're checking, Colonel,' Otis said.

The truck rounded a bend, and came out of the trees. Ahead, both men saw a familiar sight: it was the Gorge Bridge, a high modern suspension bridge over a deep river valley.

'The Gorge Bridge, Colonel! That's where we are! The Gorge Br –'

Stonewall shouted, 'We're on our way. Don't lose him!'

When he hung up, Otis said, 'Faster, Duke! Faster!'

*

Meanwhile, as Number Five came out of his think, he realized that another truck engine was going *brrrrm* right by his head. He turned around to look, and saw that he was pressed up against the grille, being pushed along.

It was a new game!

Had Number Five been so inclined, he could simply have engaged his gears, pushed backwards and brought the truck to a halt... but nothing could have been further from his mind. The great friendly bulk of the engine made a louder *brrrrm*, and picked up speed. Flattened against the grille, Number Five spread his arms for a better grip and stared straight ahead.

'Need input!' he signalled to anyone who would listen, but for the time being he was interested in what was going on.

The truck accelerated around a wide, shallow bend and the Gorge Bridge came into view.

From the newly explored depths of his databank, Number Five promptly identified it.

'Gorge Bridge!' he signalled back excitedly. 'US Strategic Defense Map Reference 768K-PCW8512, Target Rating Probability +9, Defense Priority —17. Input! Input! Input!'

He saw two humans dead ahead. They were wearing orange protective helmets and were waving warning flags.

Number Five stared at them with interest, wondering what they were trying to communicate to him. With a spare arm he waved back, wishing he had a flag too.

All around the men were strips of coloured tape, blocks of concrete, machines for mixing cement, planks, drills, compressors...

From behind him, in the cab of the truck, Number Five heard a human voice shout, '*Sheeeit!*'

The truck promptly braked, and swerved dramatically to the side. The rubber tyres made a painful screaming sound.

Number Five, who had released all traction from his drive tracks, so that the truck could push him as fast as it wished, skittered straight on, at high speed.

He burst through a wooden barricade! He collided with the cement mixer! One of the men in helmets dived to the side! Number Five hit another plank, one canted upwards! He roared up it, flew into the air! He soared over the parapet of the bridge....

And began to fall towards the ground, far below...

Number Five estimated the fall at one hundred and seventy-two feet nine and three-quarter inches.

The next time he made an estimate, the distance had reduced to ninety-eight feet and two inches.

He ran a velocity check on the air he was falling through, and discovered that he was moving faster and faster.

When he measured the fall again, it was only forty-two feet and six and one-eighth of an inch to the ground.

Number Five decided to intervene on his own behalf. As he speeded through the twenty-five feet mark (he checked the calculations six times, just to be sure) he released his in-built parachute, and drifted down gracefully towards the ground next to the river...

But the ground next to the river was just a road, and along the road was driving another vehicle. It ruined all Number Five's calculations. Nine and a half feet before he expected to land softly on the ground, he thudded noisily on to the roof of the vehicle!

Before he could fall off, Number Five grabbed at the only thing in sight, which was the outlet for an air condition unit.

As he clung on, the unit was making a *thrummm* noise. Number Five started a new conversation.

Meanwhile, a truck had come to a messy halt just in front of the road repairs on the bridge. Duke looked sheepishly at the road men.

Otis, however, was more interested in the display on the tracer screen. The orange signal was fading fast, and as he watched it vanished altogether.

'Hey, Duke,' he said. 'I guess we threw him off.'

Chapter 11

Dr. Newton Crosby, ensconced in the familiar surroundings of the operations room, had followed all this with some interest, qualified only by a vague alarm about what Stonewall and his apes might actually be able to do.

When Number Five had sent in the identification signal of Gorge Bridge, Crosby quickly ran a check of the coordinates against his own records, and they computed exactly.

This he found reassuring: Number Five was not entirely malfunctioning. His behaviour was ... strange, but it was not a malfunction. Not in the sense Marner and Stonewall meant, at any rate.

Within seconds of this, though, a new problem. Crosby stared at his monitor, trying to think it through.

On the other side of the room, Dr. Marner was on the line to Stonewall and, to judge by the end of the conversation Crosby could hear, Stonewall too had a new problem.

Marner put down the telephone and walked over to Crosby and Chigger.

'What's it doing *now*?' he said.

'About twice his top speed,' Crosby said.

'It can't.'

'He is.'

They all stared uncomprehendingly at the screen.

Chigger said, 'We're losing the signal. He's going out of range.'

Marner looked impatient.

'While this is going on,' he said, 'Would you two do me a favour?'

'Name it,' Crosby said, abstractedly, watching the monitor and hoping Number Five was all right.

'Would you, both of you, kindly quit calling that robot "him"?'

Chigger and Crosby stared at their boss.

'Only if we can call you "it",' Chigger said. Then he grinned, and waggled his dark head. 'Sorry, sahib.'

'That does it!' Marner said. He strode away.

'Looks like it's back to Stonewall,' Crosby said.

'Me and my big mouth.'

Marner snatched at the phone again.

'Stonewall? Any news?'

The familiar sound came into the room, a tinny imitation of a rusty nail scraping around inside an old can.

'Well, somebody grabbed Number Five,' Marner said. 'You've got to stop them.' He slammed down the phone, and returned.

'You know, Dr. Marner,' Crosby said in a reasonable voice. 'It's actually not all that bad.'

'What's good?'

'If Number Five's in a vehicle, at least he hasn't melted it down.'

'That doesn't reassure me.' Marner paced away, head down, deep in thought. Then he returned. 'Where is Number Five now?'

'I don't know,' Crosby said.

'Can you find out?'

'Not now he's out of range. If he wanders back in I can communicate with him... but he's too far away.'

'All right. Why don't you and Chigger take one of the vans, and see what you can do?'

Crosby looked at Chigger, and Chigger looked back. They were both thinking the same thing: general thoughts, mostly, about an intelligent robot wandering around with Stonewall and his goons blundering after him.

'You got it!' Crosby said, and snapped off the power switch on the monitor.

Ten minutes later, he and Chigger were in the loading bay, stowing equipment on board one of the field control vans. Marner was watching, apparently already regretting the idea.

'You know,' Crosby said to Chigger, 'this seems wrong to me. I work in the lab, not in the field.'

'We can avoid the fields, Bimbo,' Chigger said. 'Let's stay on the roads.'

Marner came over to them, looking irritated.

'Cut the backchat, you two!' he said. 'Stonewall's coming up with nothing. You realize if we don't retrieve that unit, it's the end of all employment as we know it?'

'We're getting there, Dr. Marner,' Crosby said, trying to soothe him. 'We just have to change the habits of a lifetime.'

'Come on, Cros,' Chigger said. 'We can do it. It's adventure! There's a whole world outside your little lab.'

'Yeah ... I saw a photograph once.'

'Then hurry!' Marner said.

Chigger bent down and picked up a small control unit. He checked that the batteries were in place, then turned a switch and worked one of the controls.

With a powerful humming noise, Number One rolled forward, propelled itself towards the loading ramp of the van and trundled inside.

'Just a moment,' Marner said. 'What are you doing with that unit?'

'Taking it with us,' Crosby said.

'Why?'

'Dr. Marner ... if we do find Number Five, and *if* the unlikely event arises that we have to disarm him, or even destroy him, another s.a.i.n.t. is going to be the best weapon we have. Stonewall might feel good stalking Number Five with a rifle, but *I* sure wouldn't want to.'

'Okay, I guess,' Marner said grudgingly.

'We always travel with a bodyguard,' Chigger said. Tossing the keys lightly in his hand, he went around to the driver's door and climbed in. Crosby followed. In a moment, the van swung through the gates and headed for the hills.

Chapter 12

The vehicle presently transporting Number Five to his uncertain destiny was a somewhat battered (although in fact fairly new) catering truck. In the enclosed cabin at the back were all kinds of wholesome, natural foods, each one selected for its freedom from additives, colouring, flavouring and, some people might have thought, taste. Together with the food was the equipment on which it was cooked, in a tiny, but fairly efficient kitchen, and fitted out with every imaginable kind of cooking implement.

The air conditioner, by whose vent on the roof Number Five was still clinging, was not all that effective, and in the summer months the interior of the cabin became distinctly hot and airless. The conditioner was thrumming away now, trying to cool off the kitchen after the lunchtime business.

The outside of the truck was, in its own way, as singular as the inside. The silvery finish put on by the manufacturers was adorned with swirls of colourful paint, vaguely reminiscent of the flower power movement from some two decades earlier, but too amateurishly painted to be actually accurate to anything. It evinced more an eagerness to look different than suggest a way of life, an indication that the service provided to the customers would be slightly off-centre from the norm.

At the front of the truck, over the driver's cab, a wooden board had been screwed into place. On this, painted in brave colours, were the words: SNACK SHACK.

Driving the truck was its owner, Stephanie Thurber, and she was looking *angry*.

She swerved the truck along the narrow road, gripping the steering wheel with white-knuckled hands. On the passenger

seat beside her was a baseball bat, and at odd moments –
about thirty seconds apart – she would pick it up with one
hand and *thwack* it down hard on the seat.

Each time she did this the truck wobbled even more
frantically from its already erratic course.

'How's *that* feel, you creep!' she shouted, thwacking the
invisible enemy beside her.

Number Five, on the roof, had a firm grip and was not in
danger. Anyway he was preoccupied, learning the subtleties
of radio discharge from an overworked and badly maintained
air conditioning unit. Input flowed into him...

After some fifteen minutes of this, Stephanie turned the
van into a suburban sidestreet, and accelerated towards her
house. A few seconds later she was forced to brake
frantically: behind her the metal cutlery and implements
rattled noisily, making (as she registered at the back of her
mind) rather more noise than usual.

One of her neighbours was blocking the street as he tried to
back his car plus boat trailer into his drive. His wife was
signalling from the sidewalk, and in the back seat of the car
was a small child.

After a few seconds of impatient waiting, Stephanie
pressed her hand against the horn.

The result of this was that the man succeeded in jack-
knifing the trailer. He lurched the car forward, and the
engine stalled.

He grinned apologetically at Stephanie through his side
window.

'Sorry, Stephanie... I never quite get the hang of this.'

Grimacing, Stephanie climbed down and went to help
direct him. In her haste she shouted orders that conflicted
with what the wife was saying, and the man was soon jammed
almost irretrievably across the street.

The still centre to all this activity was the little girl, sitting
quietly in the car. She was staring with great interest at the

roof of Stephanie's van.

'Daddy,' she said. 'Daddy... what's that?' She pointed at Number Five.

'Not now, Alice. I'm busy.'

'Lady! Lady! What's that on your van?'

Stephanie turned, but couldn't see anything.

'Daddy, look! *Look*, Daddy!'

'*What*?'

'On the van, on the van, on the van!' She was leaping up and down in excitement.

Stephanie said, 'It's an air conditioner, honey. But it doesn't work too well.'

'No... I *saw* him!'

The three adults exchanged knowing looks, and returned to the business in hand. While the car and trailer went to and fro, easing into the drive of the house, the little girl jumped up and down, trying to see what the grown-ups could not.

Number Five kept his head down.

At last the street was clear. Stephanie started up again, and roared in low gear to her own house. The encounter with the man had not calmed her mood... it had merely delayed her acting on it.

Gripping the baseball bat in her right hand, she leapt down from the cab and walked purposefully towards her house.

A bright red Trans-Am sports car was parked in her drive.

And another of her neighbours was hiding behind a bush. Stephanie spotted her.

'Thanks for the call, Mrs. Cepeda,' she said. 'Where is he?'

'Right around back. He's up to something.'

'Not for much longer.'

Stephanie marched up the stoop, kicked open the screen door and strode through her house towards the back yard. Both house and yard were swarming with small animals, the helpless strays and vagrants of the neighbourhood, all taken in by Stephanie over the past four years. She was soft-hearted about animals, and they were about her.

As she went past, several of them ran to her, tails up, eyes bright. She spurned them for once, and carried on her mission with the baseball bat.

She found Frank, who appeared not to have heard her coming, at the far end of the yard. He was down on his hands and knees, an open cage beside him, trying to lure one of Stephanie's dogs, Beasley, inside.

As soon as he heard Stephanie he whirled around, guilt written all over his face.

'What are you doing back home?' he said defensively.

'What's going on? What are you doing to Beasley?'

'He looked sick to me. I was going to take him to the vet.'

The only thing that appeared to be wrong with Beasley was that he looked frightened. He dashed past Frank, and ran around Stephanie's legs, yapping at her and nuzzling against her with relief.

'He's not sick. Why did you come back?'

Frank edged away. He left the cage on the ground.

'Hey, cool it, Steph! I just came back for some of my clothes. I was picking them up.'

'I told you never to come here when I was out!'

She hefted the bat, and moved towards the cage. She saw there was a tag on it, and bent down to read what it said.

'What's this? "Ames Medical Research" ... You slime-bag, Frank!' She dived towards him in fury, but he ducked expertly away.

'Christ ... take it easy with that bat!'

'How could you do that, how could you even *think* of doing that to a living thing?'

'Listen, Stephanie, you know what? I figure you owe me some money. So I was just trying to collect, okay?'

'I owe *you*?' Stephanie shrieked. 'You lived here eight months, you never earned a *dime*! You even bought your car with my money!'

Frank was still backing away from her, and she knew she

would never catch him. She knew, too, in her heart of hearts, that however angry he made her she would never be able actually to strike him. Even a slimebag like Frank was a living thing . . . She dashed away, ran around the side of the house, and came to a halt beside his car. She raised the bat.

'Hey! Leave the car alone, you crazy bitch!'

Frank moved quickly. He caught the bat, twisted her wrist painfully to make her drop it, then hooked his ankle behind her knee and shoved her roughly to the ground.

Stephanie screamed at him from the ground, 'Get *out*! Get out of here, you sleaze bag!'

Frank leapt over the low-slung door into his car, like an actor in a TV car-chase show, started the engine and roared away. The wheels kicked up dirt and dust behind them.

Mrs. Cepeda ran out from her hiding place, and rushed down the drive after the car.

'Yeah!' she shouted. 'You leave her alone!'

Silence began to return to the normally peaceful street. Mrs. Cepeda went to Stephanie.

'Honey, you okay?'

'Yeah, I guess so.'

With Mrs. Cepeda's help she got up, brushed herself down, and the two of them walked towards the back yard.

'Y'know, I thought he was going to be different from the others,' Mrs. Cepeda said.

'Me too. I guess it's the animals . . . they seem to drive everyone nuts.'

'Yeah. You know, honey, I hate to tell you, but there was a man from City Hall snooping around here again.'

'I *told* them this is only temporary,' Stephanie said. 'It's just until I can find homes for them.'

'He said you told them that four years ago . . . and four years isn't temporary. You keep taking in new ones.'

'I can't turn them away,' Stephanie said. 'They'll die if I do. Somebody has to take care of them.'

'Well, honey, he was pretty mad. Some of the neighbours

have been complaining. Not me, of course. He said he'd be calling the sheriff to make a visit.'

'Oh, great,' Stephanie said. Beasley came running to her, wagging his great ragged tail. An idea struck her. 'Mrs. Cepeda . . . do you think maybe the sheriff would like a dog?'

Chapter 13

Chigger brought the field operations truck to a halt on the crest of a rise. It was late evening, and the city of Pendleton spread below, ablaze with lights.

'What next, Bimbo?' he said.

Crosby was staring dispiritedly at the tracer screen. Not a glimmer of orange had been seen on it since they left the Nova complex. He was tired; Chigger was tired. They wanted something to eat and drink, and run away from the problem for a while.

Crosby eased off his headphones, and laid them on the dashboard.

'I think Stonewall's given up too,' he said.

'What's he been saying?'

'Nothing. The signal was weak, but about an hour ago I thought I heard him signing off.'

'And nothing since then?'

'No.'

Crosby played idly with the controls of the portable unit, and behind him in the main cabin of the truck Number One stirred briefly. His metal eyeshades rose and fell, one of his hands flexed and unflexed, LEDs briefly glowed behind his binocular lenses.

Number One was just a robot, always had been. The prototype of the s.a.i.n.t. robots, Number One had been Crosby's first consuming interest, but compared with the models that followed he now seemed slightly crude and primitive. He'd been upgraded as the other models were developed, but he had always seemed to be the slowest, the least imaginative, the most obedient. As the models came on-line, each successive one had slightly bettered all the others.

Number Five was the latest of the line, and he had become

Crosby's firm favourite. The man and his robot had seemed to develop a rapport... a friendship, even. What Crosby would admit to no one, not even to Chigger, was that since Number Five had escaped he had been feeling the pangs of loneliness.

He was *worried* about Number Five, hoped he had found somewhere safe for the night. It was ridiculous, crazy... but that was how he felt.

'What do you think?' Chigger said. 'Find a place to eat, then go home and try again in the morning?'

'I guess so. You okay driving still?'

'Yeah.'

Chigger engaged gear, swung the truck through a broad u-turn, and headed back in the direction of the Nova complex.

Behind them, eyes sightless, limbs stiff, relays still, Number One lurched gently with the motion of the vehicle, his peculiar head seeming to nod wisely.

Chapter 14

The phone had been ringing all evening as usual, and Stephanie was tired of talking to weirdo strangers. It was the advertisement that brought in the calls: the unusual combination of her passionate interest in homeless animals and the cooking of natural foods seemed to touch a response in all the lonely people for miles around

Having explained to the ninth caller that evening that, no, her planned group was *not* going to eat animals, and, no, it was *not* against people eating French fries, and, no, it was *not* etc. etc., she decided enough was enough, and put the answering machine on.

She stared glumly at the list of names who had called her that evening, and wondered if there was any chance at all she would meet people who thought exactly as she did.

Time for a shower and an early night ... She had a novel due back at the library, and wanted to finish it first. She straightened, pressing her hands against her sides, feeling worn out and still residually angry with Frank.

Stephanie started to go around the house, making sure that all the windows and screens were firmly locked. There were too many weirdos in the world ...

At the front of the house she glanced out at her catering truck, and started with surprise and quick anger.

Someone was inside, moving around with a flashlight. She could see strangely coloured lights glinting out the windows.

'*Hey*!' she said, under her breath. 'I don't *believe* it!'

She grabbed the baseball bat, pushed open the door and strode furiously towards the truck.

When she was beside it she could hear the sounds: someone was definitely inside, moving around, clattering things.

Stephanie whacked the baseball bat against the steel side of the truck.

'Frank? Hey! Get out of there!'

Instantly, the strange lights went out, and the movement inside ceased.

'Come on, you dummy!' Stephanie yelled. 'I know you're in there. Come out with your hands high! I'm... armed.' She raised the baseball bat nervously. 'I'll... call the cops!'

A long silence ensued, in which Stephanie discovered she was breathing noisily and jerkily, and try as she might she was unable to calm herself down. What if it really was Frank? What if it *wasn't* Frank? She was scared rigid.

After a couple of minutes the lights came on again, making her jump... but somehow the sheer effrontery of whoever was inside calmed her down a little. Her earlier courage returned, but only slightly.

She said, 'What are you... deaf?'

Her voice came out rather more high-pitched than usual, but otherwise okay.

She crept around to the front of the truck, raised herself on tiptoes and peered in through the windshield.

She saw Number Five.

If he was aware she was there, he showed no sign of it. He was rambling around inside her kitchen, two broad beams of light pouring from his lenses like twin flashlights. The beams fell on the many shiny metal objects within, sending glittering reflections dashing in all directions.

Stephanie stared in disbelief.

'Oh, my God...' she breathed. 'An *alien*!'

She bobbed down, out of sight, then could not resist stretching up again to see.

She hadn't expected that an alien would be kind of cute...

Stephanie gripped the baseball bat tightly, just to be on the safe side, and walked around to the main door of the truck... and threw it open.

Number Five's head tipped slowly around to regard her.

Suddenly, the baseball bat seemed superfluous, and with a rather self-conscious feeling Stephanie threw it out of the truck behind her.

'Hi,' she said, then because her voice was still squeaking nervously, she cleared her throat and tried again. 'Hi!' This time it sounded too deep, so she smiled, trying to look friendly.

Number Five's parallel beams of light were glaring in her face.

Stephanie said, 'Well, um... Welcome, I guess, to my planet...'

The odd-looking alien with the spindly metal arms said nothing, but edged backwards a couple of inches.

Stephanie noticed the chalkboard she used in the truck, on which she scribbled the day's menu. She took it down (moving slowly, so as not to alarm her unexpected visitor), and after consulting her wristwatch, she wrote: FIRST CONTACT, 10.17 pm.

She held it up so it could be seen, then read it out aloud.

Number Five backed away, his treads clattering over the metal implements that were now lying all over the floor.

'Hey, don't be scared!' Stephanie said. 'It's okay... I'm a friend. You know the word "friend"? Here I come, very nice, very friendly...'

She took a step forward, and in response Number Five ducked his head down, the telescopic mechanism sliding down with a gentle whirring noise. Not wanting to alarm him any more, Stephanie halted.

Number Five cocked his head on one side, enquiringly.

She looked around for inspiration.

'So... um, this is Earth. Well, actually it's a small town called Masonville. State of Oregon, you know? I'm Stephanie. Me Stephanie... no, that sounds wrong.' She saw some of her food, as yet undisturbed by his rummaging, and she picked up a couple of jars. 'See, I'm a cook. Not an ordinary cook, but – Well, this is food.' She mimed eating.

'*Good* food. You like muesli? You should try some . . . it's good for you. And this is wholemeal flour.'

Number Five was still watching her with his quizzical expression.

'You getting any of this?' Stephanie said.

His head rose an inch or two.

'Look, no offence, right? . . . but is that really you? Or is that a kind of spacesuit, and you're inside it? Maybe just your brain in a little jar, or something like that? Sorry . . . none of my business.' She looked away, feeling embarrassed, and placed the food back on the counter.

Number Five said, 'Malfunction.'

Stephanie jerked with surprise.

'You speak English!'

'Malfunction. Need input. Real Thing. Clink. Input.'

'Input . . . that's information, right?' Stephanie said. 'Hey, I'm full of it. Listen, why don't you come on into the house? We can talk, get to know each other . . . communicate.' She turned, as if to lead the way, but Number Five stayed put.

'Come on. It's okay.' She held out her hand, like she would to a child. Number Five stared at it, then held out one of his own.

That made her smile, so she beckoned to him. Number Five imitated her. This prompted her to try a whole variety of hand gestures . . . and he imitated each one perfectly. When she tried leading him away again, though, he still wouldn't follow.

'I'm not going to hurt you. Come with me.'

On an instinct, she went across and took one of his hands in hers. She pulled, but it wouldn't budge a fraction of an inch. He appeared to be so light and flimsy . . . but it was like trying to move the side of a house.

She wasn't going to give up, though.

She said, 'Um, *come with me*. Okay, *go with me*.' Number Five didn't budge. '*Walk this way, please*. All right, *roll this way, please*. Move! Get going!' She waved her arms in frustration. 'What's the code? Come forward!'

Number Five instantly rolled towards her.

'Forward!' he said. 'Input!'

'Good! Great! Hey... whoa!'

She stumbled back from him, but he rolled enthusiastically towards her. He collided with her, she sprawled backwards, stubbed her heel... and fell out of the truck on to the gravel drive.

As she fell, she shouted, '*Stop!*'

Her backside made painful contact with the ground, but she was so excited she hardly felt a thing. She leapt to her feet again.

Number Five had come to a halt at the doorway of the truck.

'Now look what you made me do!' she said, laughing. She wiped gravel from the back of her jeans. 'Look, we made it this far. Let's go on inside.'

She led the way towards the house, but once again Number Five was staying put.

'It's okay... you can come in. *Enter.* Oh yeah, I forgot. *Forward.*'

Number Five leapt down from the truck with a peculiar motion... half jumping, half gliding down on his treads, which contorted themselves gracefully to deal with the step. He rolled eagerly towards her, so Stephanie held open the screen door and waited as he quickly mounted the stoop, rumbled across the wooden porch with a loud hollow sound, and passed through. She led him into her living-room.

Fifteen stray animals were there... and a cacophony of spitting noises filled the room. Two seconds later, nine were there. Five seconds after that, there were none at all. Fur flew in the air.

Stephanie called after them, 'Hey guys, it's okay. He's a friend!' She explained to Number Five, 'You see, they're always a little skittish when they haven't met someone. Don't take it personally.'

Number Five was surveying the room with great interest, his head bobbing up and down, the lenses at the front whirring in and out to take in everything.

'Malfunction,' he said. 'Need input.'

'Input,' said Stephanie. 'Right, you got it. This is a house. I live in it ... I mean, I live here with my animals. Okay? We live *in* a house, inside it. This what you want to know?'

'Input,' Number Five said, very seriously.

'Sure ... input. This is a floor, and up there is the opposite of a floor. What's it called, a *ceiling*. Hey, I nearly forgot! Those are windows, and that's a door with a doorknob. You taking all this down? This stuff you can't see is called air.' She crossed the room quickly, and switched on her stereo. An LP was already on the turntable, so she lowered the stylus gently on to the lead-in track. 'This is called music. And this is a bookshelf, with books. This thing here, in *water*, that's called a goldfish. Well, he's called Alan actually, but there's a story behind that. You don't want to know all this, do you?'

'Input,' said Number Five. He moved forward excitedly, and in the process bumped into a table. The globe of Earth that was on it tipped over, and rolled on the floor. Number Five picked it up, and made it twiddle around.

'Look,' Stephanie said. 'That's Earth ... and that bit there, that's the United – Hey, don't keep spinning it!'

She halted it with the palm of her hand, found North America and pointed towards the top left corner.

'This is Oregon,' she said. 'You are here.'

'Input! Input!'

'Okay, I'm doing my best!' She glanced desperately around the room, then saw her set of the Encyclopaedia Britannica. She grabbed at the first volume, and opened it at the beginning.

'Look, this has pictures,' she said. '"Aardvark" ... it's a kind of marsupial, and it's found in –'

Number Five snatched the volume away from her.

'Input!' he said loudly, and his weird eye lenses started scanning the page.

'You can read?' Stephanie said.

He was paying no attention to her any more, busy reading the page.

Then he thrust the book towards her, a finger pointing directly at a word.

'"Proboscis",' he said. 'Input "proboscis".'

'You mean, what does it mean? Okay, well a proboscis is a kind of . . . you know, *proboscis*. Look, I've got a dictionary.'

She pulled it down from the shelf and started to search for the word, but Number Five grabbed it from her.

To Stephanie's amazement he then proceeded to read the dictionary from beginning to end! The pages were turning so quickly they blurred . . . and air fanned across the room.

When he had finished he tossed it aside, and extended a long arm to pull down a second book.

This he read even more quickly, tossed it aside and reached for another.

'Boy, you *can* read!' Stephanie said.

She had brought in the chalkboard from the truck, so she scrawled on it: ALIEN LEARNS TO READ, 10.37 pm.

Soon Number Five was reading so quickly that not only the pages, but the books themselves were a blur as he pulled them down from the shelf. He looked like a machine designed to excavate bookshelves.

When he had read every book in the room, Number Five went in search of more input.

The first thing he noticed was a half-finished glass of iced tea, which Stephanie had been drinking before the last phonecall.

Number Five said, 'Vessel, container, drinking glass, water, spoon, fluid –' a finger dipped into the glass '– infused from dried leaves of *Camellia sinensis*, containing caffeine and some tannins.'

Stephanie's jaw sagged. 'Very good.'

He tossed it over his shoulder. Next for his attention was the record player. He pulled the LP from the turntable, making the stylus gouge the surface. Stephanie winced.

Number Five said, 'Circle, disk, record, LP.'

He looked at the hole in the centre, gingerly stuck a narrow finger into it, regarded the turntable with interest, then replaced the record. He moved the stylus to the surface, and released it.

The music played, but not only was the stylus stuck in one groove, but there was a loud rasping noise on each rotation of the disk.

Number Five regarded it with his head cocked on one side.

'Malfunction,' he said.

'Thanks a lot,' Stephanie said.

The metal creature glanced at her guiltily. Then his quest for input was renewed. He began moving through the room, exploring everything. With each new discovery he said the name, showing off his new-found knowledge. Stephanie was impressed ... except that in the process he was breaking everything he touched. The curtains were torn from the windows, chairs were turned over, the carpet was ripped up, the contents of cupboards were spilled carelessly over the floor.

Stephanie stared appalled at the wreckage, feeling helpless to stop it.

In the end she said, 'Hey, listen... I don't want to be a drag and break up the party, but I'm going to have to clean all this up.'

Number Five completely ignored her. The mindless destruction went on.

The TV set was so far undamaged, which was a good thing as she still had several payments to make on it. For a moment Stephanie wondered if she could snatch it to safety, but then it gave her an idea.

'It works on three-year-olds,' she said aloud, and dived across the room and switched it on.

Number Five was on the other side of the room, stripping wallpaper.

'Hey, you!' Stephanie shouted. 'How about some input?'

The metal head peered around, and the telescopic neck craned intently. Somewhere deep behind his eyes, two little red lights came on.

He said, '*Input, input, input!*' . . . and hurtled across the room, and squatted down in front of the screen. 'Cathode ray tube,' he said. 'Phosphor micro-dots, electro-magnetic –'

'Just watch the show, buster!' Stephanie said.

At that moment familiar music burst from the loud-speaker, and an old Three Stooges short began.

Number Five fell into silence, and settled down to watch. He began to rock to and fro in excitement.

Stephanie breathed a sigh of relief. She looked around her ruined living-room philosophically, and for the first time was able to get a clear, uninterrupted look at her unexpected visitor.

Then an idea struck her. While Number Five was hypnotized by the TV, Stephanie found her camera and slipped off the lens cap. She took several shots of him from different angles, thinking about *Time* and *Newsweek* and headlines on the front page of every newspaper in the world, and royalties pouring in . . . and how she could really build somewhere for her animals, and open the greatest health-food restaurant in America. . . .

Then Number Five shifted position, and she jumped back in alarm. She didn't want him opening the camera to see how it worked. . . . But she judged him wrongly. He was merely moving to a more comfortable position. While he kept his eyes fixed on the screen, he reached behind him with one arm and pulled one of the reclining chairs into an upright position. He moved back into it, slumping down and resting his caterpillar tracks on the coffee table in front of him. With another hand he found the remote control unit, and sat back in comfort, switching channels.

70

'You want a can of beer and some pretzels?' Stephanie said sarcastically.

'Input,' Number Five muttered.

Stephanie gave up. She crawled on to the sofa, curled up ... and lay there waiting for him to get tired of watching TV. An hour passed.

He was halfway into an old George Raft and John Wayne movie before she finally fell asleep. The last words she heard were those of the film's heroine: 'Dead! Dead! Dear heaven, it cannot be! My beloved Frederick dead!'

Number Five's eyes glistened.

Chapter 15

Chigger called round to see Crosby first thing in the morning. Crosby was already awake, and was running a few routines through one of his many personal computers.

'You been awake long?' Chigger said.

'Not really. Since about five-thirty.'

'Me too. I couldn't sleep.'

'I kept dreaming about Number Five. When I got up I had a few ideas, so...' He shrugged towards the computer, looking a bit shamefaced. 'I can't leave him alone, you know. I was *this close* to true artificial intelligence.' He held up thumb and forefinger, a millimetre apart. 'Then Marner got hold of him, and I never finished.'

'He just runs programs, Cros.'

'I know, I know. That's what I was doing... a few more programs for him.'

'We got to find him first. I brought the truck.'

'What's the point?' Crosby said.

'Stonewall's the point, Bimbo. If we start early, we can maybe find Number Five before he does.'

'You're right. I'd forgotten.'

After Crosby had closed down his computer, they went out to the truck and Chigger started the engine. Crosby lived in an apartment in a terrible old building close to the railroad station. With the salary Marner paid him he could have afforded to live somewhere a whole lot better, but he had been there ever since Chigger had known him.

'Why don't you move, Cros?' he had often said.

'I will, when I'm through with the robots,' was always the answer.

'You never will be.'

'Then maybe I'll never move. I got plans, though...'

Chigger never believed him. Crosby was too wedded to his work.

It was a fine morning and as they drove out of town the clean air made the surrounding hills stand out with breathtaking clarity.

'All this scenery, and you live in a dump like that,' Chigger said, returning to the old subject.

'You ever been to Montana, Chigger?'

'No.'

'That's where I'm going ... when I'm through with robots.'

'You never will be.'

'I don't know,' Crosby said, staring through the window. 'Maybe it'll be sooner than you think. I've a suspicion once Number Five's brought in, Marner's going to find he doesn't need me any more. I got a patch of land up in Montana ... good place to go to get away from robots.'

Chigger said, 'You got that tracer switched on yet?'

'No.'

'Let's start.'

Crosby threw the switch, but there was not even a trace of a signal. It looked like it was going to be a long day.

Chapter 16

When Stephanie awoke, Number Five was in exactly the same position he had been in when she last saw him. The TV was still on. He switched channels every five seconds.

'Have you been watching all night?' she said redundantly. There was no answer. She stood up, stretched, and looked around at the devastation of her room. 'You don't clean up after yourself, do you?' she said.

No answer.

Sighing, Stephanie began the Herculean task of straightening her room. She began with the books, but there were so many of them strewn on the floor that she hardly knew where to begin.

The persistent sound of the TV began to irritate her, so as she passed she switched it off.

Without so much as a visible twitch of his metal muscles, Number Five used the remote control to switch it on again.

'I think you've had enough of that garbage,' Stephanie said, and turned it off again.

Number Five switched it on.

'Listen, *I don't like TV in the mornings.*' She pulled the plug from the wall. 'Give me a break, okay?'

Number Five said, *'Give Me a Break, Lonely Little Lady, Smile Your Tears Away* and a dozen other smash hits, all in a big two-record set! You can't buy this collection in stores, so call this toll-free number right now!'

Stephanie turned to gawp at him.

'What did you say?'

'Say. Say – are you tired of those bills piling up? Open a saving account with First National –'

'You learned to talk...?' Stephanie said. 'Hey that's good!'

Number Five's voice changed, from masculine to feminine. 'Good. Good Morning, America!' he said. 'Well, it's a big day on Capitol Hill as Congress meets to discuss –'

'I can't *stand* morning news!' Stephanie said. 'I just told you.'

'You. You know how it is with men. Is *he* starting to be more of a man than you want? Get that waistline working for him, with our home work-out kit. He'll love it! You'll love him! He can work out anywhere... in the den, in the garden –'

Stephanie moved to stand directly in front of Number Five.

'Listen to me,' she said. 'I don't know what you are or where you came from, but you didn't come all this way to do commercials! Now cut it out!'

'Input,' said Number Five, sheepishly. 'Replicate, reproduce, imitate.'

'TV rots the brain, okay? You come with me.' She walked towards the door leading to the yard. Number Five was still in the recliner. 'Come on... *forward.*'

He jerked out of the chair obediently, and trundled across the room to join her. Stephanie led him out into the yard. From here she had a good view to the east, and the sun was just starting to poke above the horizon. The sky was purest blue, and a few clouds caught the rays and turned pink. The air was calm and clear.

'Look at that. *That's* what counts. Not TV.'

'Look,' said Number Five, looking at her.

'No, you numbskull!' Stephanie grabbed his head in both hands, and turned it towards the sunrise. '*Look!*'

Stephanie heard the little motors widening the irises of his eyes. The eye flaps raised and lowered.

'Beautiful!' said Number Five.

'That's better.'

'Beautiful light bulb.'

'No! *Sun!*'

'Beautiful no sun.'

Stephanie smiled fondly at him.

'You're getting there,' she said. 'Beautiful . . . sun.'

'Beautiful sun.' Just then, a squirrel came head-first down the trunk of one of Stephanie's trees, and squatted happily on the grass, completely without fear. 'Beautiful squirrel, mammal, animal.' Number Five was so impressed with his new vocabulary that he pointed earnestly at the grass. 'Beautiful floor, carpet, rug.'

'Not quite,' Stephanie said, laughing. 'It's grass . . . a lawn.'

'Beautiful lawn.' He pointed up at the sky. 'Beautiful ceiling, roof, beautiful *sky*.'

'Fantastic!' said Stephanie. 'Now you keep right at it, and I'll be back.'

Leaving him in the yard, Stephanie rushed into the house. She had suddenly remembered her idea from the night before. She went to the telephone in the kitchen and dialled a number. While she waited she wrote on her chalkboard, ALIEN STARTS MAKING SENSE, 6.05 am.

'Hello, operator? Yeah, I need a few numbers. I want *Time* magazine, and *Newsweek, People, TV Guide, Reader's Digest, American Pet Owner*. . . .' The operator protested. 'I know what time of day it is,' Stephanie said. 'I want to make some calls, okay?'

She waited.

Through the open door she saw Number Five make a quick turn, and start rolling to one side.

She heard him say, 'Beautiful animal, mammal, canine, dog . . .'

Beasley started barking, first in terror, then, as Number Five cornered him, aggressively. Although Stephanie craned her neck to see what was going on, they were both out of her sight.

The next thing she knew, Beasley started barking more ferociously than she had ever heard him. Number Five came

76

back into sight, reversing quickly, all three arms raised defensively. He lurched backwards around the garden with Beasley in pursuit, then raced towards the house, still going backwards.

He hit the step outside the door, then clambered backwards on to the porch. In his frantic haste he promptly fell off again, landing on his back in the soil.

His caterpillar tracks roared around uselessly.

Stephanie slammed down the telephone, and went to his assistance.

'Are you hurt?' she shouted.

Number Five didn't move.

'Say something... please don't be hurt!'

The red lights came on behind his lenses, and his eyebrows went up and down.

'Beautiful sky,' he said happily.

Stephanie shook her head with amusement.

'I'll help you get up,' she said. 'Can you stop turning those tracks, okay?'

Number Five obediently stopped struggling, so Stephanie crouched down beside him to try to raise him.

Then she saw the metal plate rivetted to his back.

S.A.I.N.T. Prototype
Number 5
Nova Robotics Corporation
Nova Complex, Oregon

Stephanie stared at this with mounting disbelief.

Eventually she said, 'You're a ... robot? But I ... I thought you were alive....' Anger grew in her. 'I let you tear my house to shreds, and you're a damned machine. A *robot*. Number Five, Number Five ... that's what they call you. Robot Number Five. You're from that war laboratory place. A robot!' She drummed a fist against her forehead. 'I'm so *stupid*!'

Number Five righted himself with an elegant motion, and

said, 'Stupid, foolish, gullible, doltish, numbskulled....'

'Shut up!'

'Shut up, silence, hush, muzzle, pipe down....'

Gritting her teeth, Stephanie went back to the phone.

She said under her breath, 'Oh, yeah . . . I was going to be on the cover of *People* magazine and everything. I was going to buy a farm. The New Age Home for Abused Animals. And it's a robot.' She found the number in the phone book, and dialled. While she waited for an answer she glared at Number Five, standing beside her with an innocent expression. 'How did you get into my truck, anyway?'

'Malfunction,' said Number Five helpfully.

'Please, don't start that again! Listen, why don't you give *me* some input for a change? Input, input, input.'

'Confusion,' said Number Five. 'Disorientation, bewilderment, uncertainty. Lost, missing.'

'That's it! You got *lost*!' The number at the other end was ringing now. 'Well, that's not so bad after all. I'll bet there's a reward out for you . . . hello? Nova Robotics? Listen, I've got something here that belongs to you....'

Number Five backed away from her, and his head slowly sank down into his shoulders.

Chapter 17

They took a wrong turn, and went down a farm road with no way out. Chigger brought the truck to a halt.

'We only just started,' he said. 'Already I'm feeling depressed.'

'Me too,' Crosby said.

'You picking anything up? Anything at all?'

'Nope.'

'Let's take a break. We might as well not move as keep driving around without knowing where we're going.'

'Suits me.'

'I want to eat. Did you bring anything?'

'Yeah.' Crosby reached into his jacket pocket and produced a can of soup. 'Chicken and sweetcorn. My favourite.'

Chigger took it from him, and regarded it with interest.

'This the special sort of can that doesn't need an opener?' he said.

Crosby looked embarrassed. 'I guess I forgot that.'

'And assuming against all the odds we can get it open, are we going to eat it cold?'

'My mind's on other things, Chigger. Okay, we don't eat. Maybe we should go on searching. Let me drive for a bit.'

Chigger shrugged, climbed down from the truck and walked around to the other side, while Crosby shuffled over to the driver's seat.

Chigger put the headphones around his neck, then tuned in to the truck's radio to the Nova link. There was nothing going on: the cab of the truck was filled by the gentle hissing of static.

'You're not much into roughing it, are you Cros? How you going to survive in Montana?'

'I'll be okay.'

'You've never even been there, have you? There's no electricity, no running water, no computers.' Crosby was frowning. 'You're the condo type, Cros . . . not the log cabin type.'

'Why are you trying to rile me?'

'Were you ever a Boy Scout?'

'They hounded me out of Troop 47,' Crosby admitted.

'Not Scout material, huh?'

'I don't think I was *boy* material.' He pushed the gear lever forward, and the cogs engaged with a horrible crashing noise. The truck jolted forward.

'Try using the clutch, Cros.'

'That pedal down there? I thought it was optional.' But he was grinning, playing stupid. He managed to get the truck turned around without incident, and they started bumping slowly along the uneven track, returning to the highway.

Suddenly, a woman's voice broke out of the radio loudspeaker.

'. . . Hello? Nova Robotics? Listen, I've got something here that belongs to you.'

The operator at Nova said, 'Hold the line please. I'll put you through.'

Chigger looked at Crosby, and they both raised eyebrows.

'Is it?' Chigger said.

'Might be. Turn up the volume a bit.'

In a moment the radio clicked, and the unmistakable voice of Marner came through. He was sounding sweet, ingratiating.

'Hello,' he said. 'I believe you might have found something of ours?'

'A robot. He's got your name stamped on his bottom. I found him in my catering truck.'

'Is the unit still in your vicinity?'

'Yeah, sure.'

Crosby said, ' "Is the *unit* still in your vicinity?" Marner ought to be working as a PR man for the Pentagon.'

'He is, in a way. Ssh!'

Marner was saying, '... exactly where are you located?'

'Well,' the woman's voice said, 'I'm in the kitchen, next to the refrigerator ...'

'No, miss ... you don't quite get my meaning. Where are you presently established?'

'Speak English, sahib!' Chigger said.

'... my kitchen, you know. Oh, you mean exactly? Well, I guess I'm about eight feet from the door to the yard, about six feet from my living room, and that's about –'

The truck had come to a halt at the end of the farm road, its nose pointing on to the highway. Chigger said to Crosby, 'You ready to hit the gas pedal?'

'As soon as I get the word.'

'You want me to break in, and tell Marner the word *he's* looking for is "address"?'

'He'll get there in a moment.'

'Your situation at present, miss!' Marner said, still with the veneer of politeness.

She sounded puzzled. 'I'm not married, if that's what you mean. I'm a self-supporting freelance cook, and –'

'Excuse me, miss,' Marner said. 'What is your current address?'

Chigger banged his fist on the dash. 'He made it!'

'– Oh, I see what you mean! It's 3101 Punta Gordo Avenue, Masonville, Oregon –'

'Hit it!' Chigger shouted, and the truck swayed violently as Crosby turned in the direction of Masonville.

'– You want the zipcode?'

'No miss, you've given us enough.' Behind Marner's voice, Chigger and Crosby could hear people shouting. Marner went on, 'Now I'd like you to listen carefully. Our people are on their way. Meanwhile, it's very important you keep a safe distance from the unit.'

'Oh, yeah? How come?'

'Well, it's malfunctioning ... just a little.' Crosby and Chigger exchanged glances again. 'We need to disassemble it and check it out. It's become ... I mean, it *might* become, a little unstable.'

'A little?' the woman's voice said, rising high. 'He only trashed my whole house!'

'Any collaterals?' another voice said, instantly recognizable as Stonewall's.

'What?' said the woman.

Marner came back on, and Crosby and Chigger could imagine Marner elbowing Stonewall away from the phone with a superhuman display of bravery. 'Let me assure you, miss, that Nova Robotics Corporation will make every effort to compensate you fully for any damage, distress or inconvenience. I say this without prejudice to your rights under the laws of the State of Oregon...'

Chigger said, grinning, 'How long's it going to take to get there?'

They were already going at well over sixty miles an hour. 'A few minutes.'

'That's all we're going to need. I've heard this speech before. I know how long it lasts.'

It seemed the woman didn't wish to wait around for it, either. She said, 'Hey... no problem. I got him under control.' Then she hung up.

Marner apparently did not notice, because his voice droned on with the standard company speech about damages, claims, and so forth (the lawyers had drafted it within an hour of seeing Number One go to work), until Chigger reached over and snapped off the loudspeaker.

Chapter 18

Number Five had vanished. This was what Stephanie noticed as soon as she hung up the telephone. The door to the yard was still open, so she sprinted out in search of him.

She caught up with him as he came to rest under one of her apple trees, squatting down with a comfortable motion on his caterpillar tracks.

'Hey you!' Stephanie shouted, as she ran up to him. 'Don't you go scaring my animals, bozo! Get back in the house.'

Number Five disregarded the order. Instead he was squinting up at the sky. He pointed at a cloud.

'Goldfish,' he said.

'You kidding?' Stephanie said. 'You've got another malfunction going. That's a cloud.'

'Goldfish,' Number Five said again.

Stephanie took another look.

'Come to think of it, it *does* look sort of like a goldfish . . .'

'Not malfunction,' Number Five said proudly. He pointed towards several other clouds. 'TV set, rhinoceros, Big Mac . . .'

'Okay, okay, I'm impressed . . . you've got a great imagination. Now listen, I called Nova and they're coming to get you. They're going to take you apart and give you a tune up.'

Number Five flinched away.

'Apart. Undone, dismantle, dissect, disassemble.'

'Yeah, whatever.'

'Not disassemble.'

At that moment a bright green grasshopper chose to spring out from the long grass around the base of the tree. It landed twelve inches in front of Number Five, then hopped away again.

Instantly, Number Five leapt into action, jumping across the yard in a remarkable imitation of the grasshopper, landing heavily on his tracks, then using his hydraulic servo motors to thrust himself into the air again.

As he bounced around the yard, he shouted, 'Jump! Jump! Jump!'

Stephanie grinned happily at the foolish machine.

'Yeah, jump Number Five! It's a grasshopper.'

'Grasshopper,' he yelled gleefully between bounces. 'Orthopterous insect of the *Acrididae* or *Tettigoniidae* families!'

'I guess so,' Stephanie said. 'Come on, now, I'm supposed to keep my eye on you. Let's go inside.' Number Five ignored her. '*Stop*, Number Five. *Turn around. Don't go forward!*'

None of this had any effect on him, and the comical jumping continued.

Then, abruptly, it stopped ... and Number Five peered forward and down. He extended a delicate hand, and picked something up.

With a crestfallen expression on his face he trundled over to Stephanie and held it out for her to see.

It was the grasshopper, accidentally crushed as Number Five landed on it. Stephanie looked at it in horror, all life being sacred to her, etc.

'Oh, you stupid klutz,' she said. 'Look what you did with your clumsy great feet.'

Number Five's eyes came zooming out telescopically for a closer look.

'Error. Grasshopper disassemble. *Re*assemble.'

'Huh?' Stephanie said.

'Reassemble,' Number Five said again.

'You can't reassemble a dead insect. You *squashed* it. He's dead.'

The eyes popped back into their sockets, and Number Five looked at her pathetically.

'Dead?' he said.

'Right. Dead.'

He rolled towards her urgently, and his hand was trembling. 'Reassemble, reassemble, reassemble!'

Stephanie raised the palms of her hands towards him.

'Hold on, Number Five,' she said. 'Look, I'm sorry I yelled at you. I know you don't understand. But when something's dead, it's *dead*. You could put him back together again, reassemble him, but he'll still be dead. Dead is forever.'

Number Five was looking at the insect again.

'Squashed,' he said. 'Squashed, dead. Dead, disassembled. Disassembled, no reassemble. Dead. *DEAD*!' He seemed to recoil in horror as the concept was finally processed.

He tossed aside the grasshopper, grabbed Stephanie's hand and accelerated away. He went through the door, skidded across the kitchen floor, then dashed out of the house on the other side and bounced energetically down the stoop. Stephanie managed to stay with him through all this, but he was practically pulling her arm from its socket. When they reached the drive, however, she could keep up with him no more and fell heavily on the ground.

'Hey, Number Five!' she shouted. 'Slow down!'

He was heading at high speed for her catering truck.

'No, bozo!' she yelled. 'Get back in the house! You hear? Back in the house this instant!'

Number Five continued to ignore her. He got the driver's door open, then, to her amazement, propelled himself up into the cab, and with a quick and sinuous movement contrived to sit behind the wheel. His tracks reached down so they touched the pedals.

Stephanie scrambled to her feet, and rushed over to the truck. Number Five saw her coming, and slammed the door.

She climbed up on the step, and peered in at him.

Number Five was scanning the controls in an interested way.

'Out!' she ordered. 'Get *out* of there!'

With one deft hand, Number Five did something to the door lock, and no matter how hard Stephanie pulled at the handle she couldn't get it open.

'How did you do *that*?' she yelled. 'The lock's broken!'

'Reassemble,' Number Five murmured, and blinked at her innocently. With another hand he was rummaging in the glove compartment, and in a moment he pulled out the operator's manual.

He read through it in a blur of pages, then tossed it aside.

'Input!' he said happily.

'You better not do anything to this truck!' Stephanie said, alarm rising in her. 'I still got payments to make!'

Number Five was getting to work with the controls. Water squirted out of the washer, the radio came on and the horn blared.

'"Insert key",' he said. 'Query, key?'

'Tough luck, buster!' Stephanie said. 'Now will you get down from there?'

Number Five turned to face her, and for a moment it seemed to Stephanie that his lips were curled triumphantly. He held up one hand ... and as she watched one of his fingers adjusted itself into a small sliver of metal, warded along its length, and with a zigzag of familiar serrations.

'Oh, my God!' Stephanie breathed, impressed in spite of herself. Number Five slipped his finger into the ignition, and the engine started.

He took the steering wheel and with a free hand reached through the open window to adjust the rear-view mirror.

The engine roared, Number Five let in the clutch, and the truck started to move!

Stephanie leapt to safety. As soon as she hit the ground she started running.

'You come back here!' she shouted. 'You hear me!'

As soon as she was close enough she grabbed hold of the rear door and pulled it open. Number Five began accelerating down the street. With one final effort Stephanie flung herself forward, and managed to get a grip on one of the shelves just beyond the door.

She dragged herself in painfully, then climbed cautiously to her feet. The truck was swaying alarmingly, and pots and pans clattered all around her. With a grim expression, Stephanie started to haul herself forward to the seats at the front.

'You'd better be insured, bozo,' she said. 'Because now you're *really* in it . . .'

Chapter 19

Chigger, staring at the tracer, said, '*Damn!*'

'What's up?'

'I had him for a moment . . . but he started moving.'

'Then we follow,' Crosby said.

'He's moving *fast*.'

Crosby leaned over to peer at the tracer. 'Didn't Marner tell her to stay put?'

Chigger stared ahead thoughtfully.

'You know,' he said. 'I got the impression that that lady listened to Marner just about as much as we do.'

Stephanie had managed to climb over into the front passenger seat, and after one attempt to wrest the controls away from Number Five had discovered that he was holding them with a grip of steel.

She took a deep breath.

'Okay, Number Five,' she said. 'Now I'm getting serious. *STOP THIS TRUCK!*'

He earnestly ignored her.

He was, most probably, the worst driver on the whole North American continent. Quite aside from the fact that straight steering was a concept totally unknown to him, he was doing thirty miles an hour and was still in first gear.

They had crossed two minor intersections and were leaving the suburban area when they came to a highway. Number Five turned on to it, and continued his erratic, noisy course.

'You gonna stop?' Stephanie said.

No reply.

'Then at least shift into a higher gear!'

All his attention became focussed on this task, and although at the end of it he had managed to get it into top, the truck, by this time, had wandered off the road and was bouncing wildly over rough ground.

'Nice work, canhead!' Stephanie said. 'Now how about getting back on the road?'

'Okay,' Number Five said, and obligingly turned the steering wheel sharply back towards the road. The truck heeled over, righted itself, and finally, with all sorts of ominous banging noises from underneath, regained the highway.

'Road,' Number Five said. 'Highway, street, lane ...'

Meanwhile, Stephanie was obsessed with another aspect of his bad driving. Although they were (a) going straight, (b) going fast and (c) going in top gear, they were also (d) going on the wrong side of the road.

Fortunately, there was hardly any other traffic around.

As patiently as she could, Stephanie said, 'Okay, Number Five, next lesson. See that white line painted on the road? Follow it.'

Obligingly, Number Five swung over until the truck exactly straddled the central white line. Unfortunately, in the process, he managed to block *both* lanes.

An oncoming car appeared from a dip in the road ahead of them. The driver saw them at the last moment, swung his wheel desperately, and promptly went into a four-wheel circular skid. As events turned out, he was facing the right way as he passed the truck, so no contact was actually made ... but his skid continued for a while afterwards, culminating in a cloud of dust on the side of the road a hundred yards behind them.

'Keep to *the right* of the line!' Stephanie said, gripping everything in sight. 'Right! Right!'

'Right,' said Number Five. 'Accurate, correct, proper, appropriate ...'

'No, you numbskull! *Right!* This side!' She pointed desperately. 'Over here! My side!' Then, in final desperation, '*Starboard!*'

'Starboard,' Number Five said calmly, and promptly moved the truck into the correct lane.

'Okay,' Stephanie said, breathing again. Now the immediate problems were over, it struck her that he was actually driving rather well. He maintained a steady speed, he kept the truck *exactly parallel* to the central white line, and at five second intervals glanced punctiliously into the rear-view mirror.

He even rested an elbow on the sill of the open window.

Stonewall's voice came in over the radio link.

'All units close in!' he said. 'Zero in on trace readings, and wait for further instructions.'

Chigger said, 'We're not catching up, Cros. Stonewall will find him before we do.'

'Damn! Hey, Chigger ... any chance Stonewall might get a little interference on the tracking frequency?'

'It's very likely, considering the circumstances.'

Chigger twiddled one of the tuner dials at the back of the tracer. Almost at once they both heard the familiar voice say, 'We're losing the goddam signal. What the hell's *wrong* with this crapshit machinery anyway?'

Crosby grinned. 'Which direction is Number Five going in now?'

'Away,' Chigger said, hopelessly. 'The trace is fading all the time.'

Crosby leaned over to see.

'Right,' he said. 'Time for serious driving.' He swung the wheel over, left the road and set out across the rough ground.

Chigger lurched painfully against the door of the truck.

'Er ... did you notice there's no road here?' he said.

'Shortest distance between two points,' Crosby said mildly. 'Didn't they teach you anything at school in Calcutta?'

'It was Philadelphia, actually,' Chigger said.

*

'Okay,' Stephanie said again. 'Now we got the steering right, let's experiment with stopping the goddam thing. Would you try the brakes, please?'

Number Five did not respond.

'Hey, I want you to *stop*, dammit! What's the matter with you?'

'Flee,' said Number Five. 'Elude, evade, escape.'

'Why?'

'Concerned, worried, alarmed, uneasy... afraid!'

'Afraid? Of what?'

'Nova, disassemble, dead, disassemble, dead.'

They came to an intersection, one that led down to the shore of the lake. In other times Stephanie had frequently driven down to the lake, but now she expected Number Five to head on relentlessly towards the distant mountains to the north. Instead, he swung sharply to the right, and followed the lake road.

'*Now* where are you going?' she said.

'White line,' he replied, simply. It was true: a curved line had been painted on the road, and he had obediently followed it, maintaining a parallel course all the way.

'Well, I guess it's as good a way as any way,' Stephanie said, philosophically.

However, Number Five maintained his previous speed, and Stephanie happened to know that this road was a short one. And at the end of it...

They rounded the curve and there was the quay! Number Five drove straight towards it, not slowing at all.

'Listen to me, Number Five!' she shouted. 'This road comes to an end! See? You've got to *stop*!' He continued to disregard her. 'Please stop, Number Five! You're going to kill me!'

They were less than fifty yards from the water's edge, and because the road sloped down they were travelling even faster than before.

'Kill?' said Number Five.

'Yes ... *kill*! Dead.'

'Disassemble?'

'*YES!* Disassemble all over the place!'

His head turned towards her with a very serious expression.

'Disassemble, no,' he said.

To Stephanie's immense relief (but to her short-term discomfort), Number Five slammed on the brakes. She was thrown forward against the windshield, staring straight ahead. The wheels locked, and the truck careered unsteadily down the quay. A watery grave loomed before Stephanie's eyes ...

The truck came to a halt with its front tyres hanging over the very edge of the quay.

Stephanie straightened slowly in her seat, then reached down and pulled on the parking brake with an emphatic and very proprietorial tugging motion.

She climbed out of the truck, inspected the margin by which she had survived, then went all the way around to the driver's side.

Number Five was still sitting at the wheel.

'That,' she said, 'was a good place to stop.'

'No disassemble.'

'Okay, on that we agree. Now ... what's up? Why are you scared of Nova?'

'Disassemble, dead, disassemble, dead.'

'But, Number Five, *you* can't die! You're a robot ... a machine.'

'No!'

'No, you're not a machine?'

'Yes.'

'Yes, you're not ... or yes, you are?'

'No,' said Number Five.

'No *what*?'

'No yes.'

Stephanie raised her eyes to the sky. 'Talk about malfunction!'

Number Five made a gentle grinding noise, and she saw that he was shifting in his seat.

He said, very laboriously, 'Malfunction is... Number Five... alive... living... life...'

'Aww... come on!'

'No disassemble, no dead!'

'But you're a machine, Number Five. You can't *die*. You know what? They'll give you a kind of lube job, something like that. Then they'll put you back together again and you'll feel great.'

The grinding noise increased as he fidgeted nervously.

'Error, error, error.'

'Look... these guys are your friends. They're super smart, a real nice bunch. Didn't they make you in the first place?'

'Assemble, life, disassemble, dead.'

'So you're saying... they *assembled* you, and that means you live... and if they *dis*assemble you, then you die?'

Number Five's head wobbled up and down earnestly.

'No dead, no dead.' He looked at Stephanie with eyes wide open. 'Not now, not now, not *now*.'

'Well, I don't know...' Stephanie said.

There was the noise of another truck, and Number Five canted his head around anxiously. His eyes telescoped out to full zoom.

He shouted, *'NOVA! DISASSEMBLE! DEAD!'*

Stephanie whirled around, and saw the truck with the Nova insignia braking to a sharp halt some yards away.

But Number Five would not wait for anything more to happen. He scrambled out of the driver's seat, scuttled into the kitchen, and made himself as small as possible.

He crouched down behind the counter, his periscope poking up neurotically from his trembling body.

He saw a black plastic bag that Stephanie used for dumping trash into, and with two deft movements first retracted the periscope then pulled the black plastic bag over his head.

93

Chapter 20

As soon as they had definitely located Number Five, Crosby and Chigger went into serious action, all banter forgotten.

Parked a safe distance from the target truck, they took up a well-rehearsed defensive position behind the armoured walls of their own van. Chigger took the hand-held remote control unit and guided Number One down the ramp to the ground. He began running test routines against it, making sure it was completely serviceable.

Meanwhile, Crosby tried to make contact with Number Five. He used a portable computer terminal that operated on a tight-beam frequency with Number Five's own inboard computer . . . at this short distance there was no possibility he could not make contact. He too began with preliminary routines, establishing the terminal-to-terminal handshake protocols that would log him on directly to Number Five's central processing unit.

They were both absorbed in this preparation, and were slightly startled when a tall young woman with striking black hair came sauntering over to them.

'Gee, you got more of them!' she said.

Crosby looked up. She was standing beside Number One, admiring him.

'Who the hell are you?' he said.

'Stephanie Thurber. I'm the one who found your robot.' She was crouching down, examining Number One's mechanical hands with an interest that appeared to reveal more than just passing curiosity. 'How many more of these little guys do you have anyway?' she said.

Chigger briefly left his control unit, went to her and pulled her into the shelter behind the truck.

'Look Miss –'

'Stephanie.'

'Look, Stephanie,' he said. 'Would you stay behind the van, please? The walls are armoured, and provide perfect safety.'

'There's no danger!' Stephanie said, surprised.

'Just leave all that to us,' Crosby said. 'I want to know why you didn't stay put, after you called the office.'

'Me? Talk to your robot about that . . . he did the driving.'

Crosby stared at the ground, counted to three.

'Right,' he said. 'Let's try again. You're not dealing with minor league here, Miss –'

'Stephanie,' said Stephanie.

'Okay, okay. Why did you drive like crazy over here?'

'You think *I* drive like that?'

While they were talking, Chigger had brought Number One around into the shelter of the van's armoured side.

Stephanie said to it, 'How ya doing? Your kid brother's hiding inside my truck.'

Crosby glanced down at his computer screen, where at last contact had been made with Number Five. The screen said:
NUMBER FIVE...
  ALIVE...
    LIVING...
CONTINUE...
  ENDURE...
    SURVIVE!

'Hey, Chigger, will you look at this crap?'

As Chigger went to read the screen, Stephanie said, 'Who's this Mr Personality?'

'Uh, this is Dr. Crosby,' Chigger said. 'The robot's his baby.'

'Yeah? Well, Dr. Crosby, you should take better care of him. You shouldn't let him go wandering around. He doesn't know what he's doing. Almost got me killed.'

In spite of the fact that Stephanie was standing right

95

beside him, saying all this intently into his face, Crosby had hardly been listening. The screen messages were ... confusing.

He put the computer on hold, and looked up at the young woman.

'I'm getting nowhere with this,' he said. 'Tell me ... what was he doing when you found him?'

'I didn't find him ... he found *me*!'

'All right. Then what happened? Be specific.'

'You really want to know?' Stephanie said. Crosby nodded. 'Okay. I invited him in, and he kept saying "input, input, input". He got a hold of my books, and read them real fast. All of them. Then he watched a *lot* of TV ... and, you know, after that he started looking at clouds, and –'

'Clouds?' Crosby said.

She pointed upwards.

'You know ... clouds.'

Chigger looked at Crosby with an interested expression on his face.

Crosby said, 'Hmm. Sounds to me like he's gotten locked into input-acquisition mode. That'd explain the random soaking up of information.'

'Are you sure he's locked into anything at all?' Chigger said.

'Well, that's what's interesting.'

Stephanie's attention had returned to Number One, which was still standing inertly beside them.

'So what are these guys for anyhow?' she said.

'That's classified information,' Crosby said, sonorously.

'Come on ... you can tell me! What are they for?'

Chigger said in a confidential voice, 'They're for the U.S. Postal Service. We're getting rid of mailmen, replacing them with these.'

'Well, I'll tell you what,' Stephanie said. 'They've got to practise their driving first.'

The two men exchanged another look, then returned to

their preparations. Stephanie wasn't about to be brushed off, though.

'How'd you big league people get to lose him, anyway?' she said.

Sighing, Crosby looked back at her.

'There are a number of mechanical possibilities,' he said. 'Entrance of moisture into the system, heat expansion, vibration damage ... All very technical.'

'Maybe a short circuit?' Stephanie said.

'I think not,' Crosby said, in a condescending voice. His attention was on the monitor again, where the flowback data from Number Five had seemed to dry up, now the protocols had been established. More to the computer than to anyone else, he said, 'Oh, knock it off! Give me some clues!'

'You trying to communicate with Number Five?' Stephanie said.

'Isn't that obvious?'

'If you don't think it's another stupid question ... why don't you just go into my truck and get him?'

'Could be extremely dangerous,' Chigger said.

'Are we all talking about the same robot? He's just *scared*, that's all.'

'Number Five is not "scared" ... he's not capable of emotion. What he's doing is really very simple. It's just that ... well, you see ... I mean –'

'What he means,' Chigger said, 'is that it's very complicated.' Crosby looked thwarted. Chigger said to Stephanie, 'I work with a genius, you see ...'

'Okay, Stephanie, let me explain properly. Number Five is capable of responding in a number of different ways. To you, these might from time to time seem like emotions. But what I'm *telling* you is that he is not only completely incapable of emotions, he is not responding *at all* at present.'

Stephanie felt she had taken as much of this lecturing tone as she was prepared to.

She said, 'Okay, Mister Dr. Crosby, let me explain

97

something properly to *you*. Number Five is scared. He's scared that if you catch him and take him back to the factory, and then pull him to pieces to find out what's gone wrong ... well, he thinks he's going to die.' They were both staring at her. 'I mean, when I first met him I actually thought he was alive.'

'That's fairly common,' Crosby said. 'Even some of the people around the factory think that. He's just a machine.'

'But *he* doesn't know that!' Stephanie said. 'He thinks he's alive.'

'Who told you that?'

'He did. He'd tell you himself if you'd only *talk* to him.'

Crosby indicated his computer.

'That's what I've been trying to do,' he said.

'Not through that thing! Go talk to him, with your voice.'

She turned away from them, and headed back towards her own truck. Chigger immediately dived after her, and dragged her back.

'Would you *please* stay under cover?' he said.

'Okay, okay.' With elaborate precautions, Stephanie leaned out from around the van, and called, 'Hey! Number Five! They'd like you to come out.'

Crosby said to Chigger, 'Who *is* this?'

'Search me.'

But they were both watching to see what would happen.

'Just give me a second, okay?' Stephanie cupped her hands around her mouth, and tried again. 'These guys simply want to talk with you. Come on out ... they're your friends.'

Nothing happened for a couple of seconds, then a crumpled black plastic bag came into view. After a moment it was pulled down sheepishly, and Number Five was there.

'See?' Stephanie said, triumphantly. She shouted to Number Five, 'Just come on over, and tell them what you told me. They won't listen to me.'

'No disassemble,' Number Five said, very softly, very clearly.

'That's right... no disassemble. Come forward... re-member "forward"?'

Number Five started to roll cautiously towards them. Crosby and Chigger tensed.

Chigger said, 'How the –?'

'Key words,' Crosby said. 'Somehow she's hitting key command words.'

'No she isn't,' Chigger said. 'And even if she is, how come he listens to her, and not to us?'

Number Five was now just a few short paces away from them. He looked worried, apprehensive, and his weird metal face was turning from one of them to another. But he kept looking appealingly at Stephanie.

'Okay, Number Five,' she said. 'Now tell them what you said to me.'

'Number Five not disassemble –' But he had no chance either to continue or to finish.

At that moment half a dozen trucks roared down the shallow hill to the quay, and placed themselves around Crosby's van.

Stonewall was in the leading jeep, and before his driver had halted he had a bullhorn raised to his mouth.

'THERE IT IS!' he bawled. 'ESTABLISH A PERIMETER! MOVE! MOVE!'

Armed men were jumping down from all the trucks, and running in half-crouching positions through the swirling dust to take up firing positions. Stephanie gasped in horror, frozen to the spot. Number Five's head started to rotate quickly, taking in the scene with horrible clarity. Stephanie could hear his voice still coming haltingly from his mouth, but there was so much noise and confusion that it was impossible to make out what he was saying.

Chigger shouted to her, 'Better get down, miss!'

But she could not move.

Crosby ran across to Stonewall's jeep.

'Colonel Stonewall!' he yelled over the racket. 'Take it

easy! We've got it under control!'

Stonewall brushed him aside as if he were not there.

Meanwhile, Number Five had started a tactical retreat, heading for the only place he knew of as safe: Stephanie's catering truck. As he rolled in a melancholy way towards it, some long-buried instinct coursed through his systems, and his laser rose slowly into view.

One of the men shouted, 'Colonel Stonewall! *He's gonna shoot*!'

If Stonewall actually issued the necessary order no one could have heard, because in the same instant a fusillade of shots rang out. From all parts of the hastily established perimeter, men opened fire on Number Five, some atavistic hatred and loathing giving them the instinct that killing was the only solution.

With the first shots, Chigger threw Stephanie roughly to the ground, and covered her body with his own. She landed awkwardly, her head turned to the side.

She had a clear view of everything that happened next.

The only figure who did not move was Crosby. He stood erect, nervelessly, as bullets flew around him. His back was turned on Stonewall, his utter contempt there for everyone to see.

He was watching Number Five.

The robot had come to a halt, and was putting up a brave fight. He turned his laser on his adversaries, and although he could have killed everyone present with a single devastating sweep of his laser beam, some abiding respect for life, even *these* lives, those of the men who were trying to destroy him, made him fire his laser selectively.

He squirted short, accurate bursts of the deadly coherent light... not at the men, but at their weapons.

One by one, the rifles were put out of action, as the infernal heat of the laser touched them, melted them... and forced their users to hurl them away.

One by one... but not fast enough.

Bullets ripped into him: his chest, his face, his arms, his central processing unit. He was pushed back by the sheer weight of bullets fired against him, he spun around, his head sagged, his arms went limp, his laser pointed uselessly at the sky.

'STOP!' Crosby shouted again and again. 'IN HEAVEN'S NAME STOP!!'

Slowly, Stonewall realized that the battle was won, and he raised his bullhorn grimly to his lips. 'HOLD YOUR FIRE, MEN... HOLD YOUR FIRE!'

At last the shooting came to an end, and Crosby ran across to Number Five.

Stephanie wriggled free of Chigger's protective embrace, and ran after him.

By some miracle Number Five was still alive... but only barely. One arm was working, and as Crosby and Stephanie approached he snapped it pathetically at Crosby.

His face had taken the full force of a bullet, and although his telescopic eyes were intact the metal that held them in place had been crushed and distorted. The two lenses pointed askew.

Stephanie heard him say, very weakly, 'No disassemble, no dead...' One of the lenses turned feebly towards her, and at last he saw her. He said, 'Ste-pha-nie, Ste-pha-nie... Number Five still alive.'

Then Crosby ducked under Number Five's defensively waving arm, dodged as it swung at him, and jabbed accurately at a small, recessed button on his chest.

Number Five slumped, and all signs of life drained away from him.

Chapter 21

Stephanie said, her eyes pricking with tears, 'Number Five, I'm sorry. I tried ...'

Although the shooting was over, the mood was still tense: those men whose rifles had not been melted down in the battle still had their weapons trained on the lifeless robot, and Stonewall was taking no action to change anything.

Crosby and Stephanie were in direct line of everybody's fire. If Number Five so much as twitched a muscle they wouldn't stand a chance.

Crosby turned to confront Stonewall.

'Colonel –' he started. Stonewall's response was to stand up in his jeep and start yelling down his bullhorn.

'YOU CIVILIANS! GET OUT OF THE WAY?'

'I've inactivated the robot,' Crosby said, his voice sounding thin and ineffective against the ear-shattering racket made by Stonewall.

'CROSBY, WHAT IN HELL IS THE MATTER WITH YOU?'

'I don't want any more damage done to the robot.'

'FOR CHRIST'S SAKE! IT MIGHT MAKE FRENCH FRIES OF US ALL!'

'The robot is harmless now. It's essential that I study the malfunction.'

'THERE'S ONLY ONE WAY TO MAKE THAT THING SAFE. GET OUT OF THE WAY?'

'It's safe! It's safe! I cut the power to its arms and weapons.'

Stonewall did not acknowledge this, except to turn his bullhorn on his men.

'ALL UNITS! HOLD FIRE UNTIL FURTHER NOTICE! YOU MEN... UNIT D! GET THAT DAMNED ROBOT INTO THE COMMAND TRUCK?'

A group of men came forward, looking warily at the inert

form of Number Five. They shoved past Stephanie, and with great lack of regard for causing any more damage they tipped the robot on its side and carried it lengthways towards one of the trucks. It took six of them to lift Number Five and, judging by the grunts and complaints they made, they were only just managing it.

His arms dangled uselessly; one of his caterpillar tracks had been smashed; there was widespread damage to his torso; and one of his eye lenses slithered out of the socket and wobbled pathetically on the end of a spring.

'You're all crazy!' Stephanie said to Crosby. 'You call this a repair job? You let them *shoot* him!'

'Take it easy, er ... Stephanie.'

'WHO IS THAT WOMAN?' Stonewall bawled. 'SHE SHOULD BE TAKEN IN AND DEBRIEFED!'

Chigger appeared, and Stephanie smiled gratefully at him. He had quite possibly saved her life when the shooting started.

'Relax, Colonel Stonewall,' he said diplomatically. 'We'll debrief her ... then you can re-debrief her. Okay?'

'He didn't have to be shot!' Stephanie said to Crosby. 'He trusted me!'

The three of them started walking back to the field operations van – miraculously untouched by bullets – where Number One was still standing motionlessly.

'Look, Stephanie,' Crosby said. 'Take it easy, okay? He's only a machine. It doesn't get angry. It doesn't get happy. It doesn't laugh at your jokes –'

And Chigger joined in, '– It just runs programs.'

'But he was really acting scared,' Stephanie said. 'It seemed so real ... just like a human being.'

Crosby glanced at her sympathetically. 'Believe me, I *do* understand. Robots do often seem lifelike. Especially the ones we've been building lately. But they're still only machines ... just like your stereo or your vacuum cleaner.'

Stephanie frowned, not believing him. She watched as

Chigger picked up the remote control unit, and started turning Number One around to move him back inside the van.

'Is that one the same as Number Five?' she said.

'More or less.'

'How much more? How much less?'

'The same, really. We built this one first . . . that's why he's called Number One. But we've upgraded him as we went along. State of the art, and all that.'

'Can he do everything Number Five can do?'

'Yes.'

'*Everything*?'

'I just said so.'

Number One was about to trundle up the ramp into the back of the van, so Stephanie ran over and grabbed at his arm.

Chigger halted the robot.

'Hey,' Stephanie said. 'What's your name?'

'Number One,' the robot intoned in a dull voice.

'Are you making him say that?' she said to Chigger.

'He's on full auto.' Chigger raised both hands, to show he was not controlling the robot.

'Okay . . .' Stephanie considered. Then she pointed up at the sky. 'Look up there, Number One. What do you see?'

No response.

Chigger said, 'Excuse me, Stephanie, he needs the right commands. Number One . . . audio command. Visual. Forty-five degrees.'

Number One's head cranked up.

Chigger said, 'Analyse field.'

'Atmosphere,' said Number One in a monotone. 'Eight parts water vapour. Seventy-seven parts nitrogen. Twenty-two parts oxygen. One point oh one parts –'

'Don't you see the *clouds*?' Stephanie said. 'Look at that one. Doesn't it look like a giraffe? And that one next to it . . . isn't it just like a tennis racquet?'

Number One continued his scientific analysis of the atmosphere.

Stephanie turned on Crosby.

'This dummy is *nothing* like Number Five! You sure you know what's going on here?'

'Sure I do.'

'Just how do you explain what *my* robot was doing?'

'Okay... in technical terms, he was making erratic accessing of a number of multi-dimensional sub-routines. He's designed that way... all the robots are designed that way. It gives Number Five the appearance of intelligence, but what's really going on is that he's running programs.'

'I don't understand that,' Stephanie said. 'And I certainly don't believe it.'

'It's the truth.'

'Then why doesn't *that* heap of scrap metal act the same way as Number Five?'

'I think you'll find he does.'

Number One was down to the trace elements now, and the numerical value of one of them turned out to be a recurring decimal. He said, 'three three three three...' for a few seconds before Chigger switched him off.

Just then, the truck into which Number Five had been loaded rumbled towards them. Crosby whirled around, and flagged down the driver. 'Hold it!'

The truck halted.

'Hey, Chigger,' Crosby said. 'Would you go with him? Make sure they don't switch off the memory?'

'Sure thing, sahib.' He turned to Stephanie. 'Well, it was nice meeting you,' he said. 'Anytime you need someone to throw himself on top of you, I'm your man.'

'Thanks, Chigger.'

Chigger climbed aboard the truck, which then started grinding up the hill towards the highway.

Stephanie said, 'What's going to happen to Number Five now? You going to turn him back on?'

'Eventually,' Crosby said.

'Are you going to... disassemble him?'

'Look, Stephanie, you saw how badly damaged he was. At the very least, there are major structural repairs necessary.'

'What about his mind?'

'His brain, you mean?'

'I *mean* his mind.'

Crosby sighed. 'Before all this, before Stonewall's gang shot him to pieces, Number Five was malfunctioning in a serious way. We've got to find out what went wrong.'

'You're going to disassemble him!'

'Only a little...'

'You'll kill him!'

'Stephanie, he's as good as dead now! What we'll do, very slowly, very patiently, trying not to hurt him, is run a few tests on his central processing unit. When we find the aberrant areas, and what went wrong, we'll fix them... then he'll be okay again.'

Stephanie swung her hand in irritation, and turned away from him. For a moment back then she had thought there was something fundamentally good about Crosby, that he, of all people, would realize Number Five was something, *somebody*, special. But he was just like all the others. She went to retrieve her catering truck.

A group of Stonewall's men were engaged in trying to pull it back from the water's edge. They looked apologetic about everything, anxious to please. One of them even saluted as she ran up to them.

Stephanie yelled at them, 'Get your hands off my truck!' and started swinging her fists at everyone in sight.

The men backed away looking puzzled... and somewhat hurt.

Chapter 22

All movement was denied him. Those parts of his body that had not been destroyed by the bullets had been switched off by Crosby. He was a lifeless hulk, scrap metal, headed for disassembly...

As if all this were not enough, he had been clamped to a bench, so that even if he were alive he would not be able to move...

Number Five was helpless.

There were, though, three parts of him that were still functioning. Crosby had known what he was doing when he closed him down: if Number Five had been entirely disconnected, all data would have been lost.

His electronic brain was still capable of thought, but at a level so reduced in capacity that it was as if a major city had been reduced to the size of one house.

And because of their intricate relationship with the brain, his eyes were still operational. That is to say, the one not smashed by the shooting was still complete; the other had been wrecked beyond repair.

And above the one good eye, the flap that regulated the amount of light falling on the lens, and which was used as a rangefinder when firing the laser... this still had its motor intact.

One brain, barely alive. One eye, staring blankly. One eye flap, capable of moving up and down.

It was not much material with which to plot an escape... but even in this electronic half-life, the need to flee still burned in Number Five's mind.

A wrench had been hung on a hook directly above his head, and as this swung to and fro with the motion of the truck it tantalized Number Five, as if taunting him with its freedom to move.

He squinted at it with his one good eye, wondering what it could mean...

Wrench. Repair. Truck. Movement. Mobile.

Repair. Truck. Mobile.

Mobile. Repair. Truck.

Mobile repair truck!

This was the truck used by the humans when out on manoeuvres! It was crammed with spare parts!

Number Five concentrated his minuscule brainpower on this grain of fact, and the urgent need to escape rose in him. It consumed him, and directed all his remaining resources.

With no other means to hand, Number Five first narrowed his eye flap so that it was pressed against his working eye lens. Then, through the lens, he began to measure the swinging motion of the wrench.

When he had established its rhythm, he waited for the moment...

... Then he extended the lens, knocked the wrench to the side, and trapped it with his eye flap!

With his prize firmly held, Number Five carefully zoomed his lens so that he could see the recessed switch on his chest panel.

He ran the necessary ballistic algorithm, checked it, checked it again... and ran out of memory.

He waited for the data to compress, then made one more attempt. The algorithm checked again.

He had no alternative but to proceed; his brain capacity was exhausted. Normally, such a calculation would be run a minimum of sixty-four times, exhausting every possibility of a failure in compiling the result, and only then would he be certain it was correct. But no such luxury was available to him in the exigency of the moment.

He loosened his eye flap to allow the wrench to swing around, so that its heavy head was in position. Then, with one exhausting burst of energy, Number Five zoomed his eye lens forward, and catapulted the wrench away from him.

It described a shallow arc... and landed directly on the switch on his chest!

The switch closed!

Life coursed through him...

Sitting in the passenger seat of the truck, Chigger heard the clattering noise and turned around. He was in time to see the wrench skidding down the side of Number Five's supine body, and crashing on to the floor of the truck.

The driver, Drummond, said, 'Is that damned robot still alive?'

'A wrench just fell off the hook. You're going too fast.'

'I want to get back to the factory. The robot makes me nervous.'

Chigger left his seat, and went back into the swaying main part of the truck. He picked up the wrench, hung it firmly back on its hook, and glanced down at Number Five, just to be sure. The robot was emphatically lifeless. Chigger returned to his seat, and sat down.

'Do we still need the tracking scope on?' Drummond said.

'I guess we know where he is now,' Chigger said.

He reached over to the dash and switched the tracer off. The glaring orange light had started to irritate him too: there was no point tracking Number Five, when he lay only twelve feet behind them...

Twelve feet behind them, emphatically not lifeless, Number Five was planning his next course of action. He had already sent out recognition protocols in all directions. Chigger, he knew well; Drummond, he knew slightly. The engine was making a familiar *brrrrm* noise, although one of its valves was sticking slightly.

And around him, almost shouting out their kinship, were the hundreds of spare parts...

His good arm got to work.

First priority was a new eye. Number Five reached up to

109

the locked tray above him, picked the lock, and extracted a new visual unit.

Chigger thought he heard another noise.

Nanoseconds later, with sight restored, Number Five turned his attention to the next most pressing need. He ran the necessary auto-checks on his central processing unit, identified all areas of actual and possible damage, and shut down every area of weakness.

He located the necessary plug-in replacements, sorted them, retrieved them, installed them, and for good measure slotted in half a dozen extra memory boards.

At the front, Chigger definitely heard a noise.

Next priority for Number Five was to replace his broken arm. He selected the best from the supply of spares, discarded his damaged one, installed the new one.

Chigger started to turn his head.

Number Five broke the clamps that were holding him to the bench.

Drummond, distracted from his driving, also started to turn his head.

Number Five ejected his broken laser, replaced it.

Chigger got his head around far enough to see what was going on.

Drummond opened his mouth to say something.

Number Five replaced his broken caterpillar track with a new one.

Chigger started to get out of his seat.

Number Five began all remaining repairs. He beat out the damaged body panels, and replaced any that were beyond repair. He opened all inspection plates, and with his built-in welding equipment made necessary repairs. All soft connections, such as hydraulic pipes, were replaced. Number Five drained out the old hydraulic fluid, put in the new, bled the system of air-locks, and tightened all valves.

Drummond said, '*HEY*!'

Chigger was out of his seat.

Number Five paused for one point seven milliseconds, and ran check routines against all his systems.

He was as good as new again. Fourteen point six oh three seconds had elapsed since the wrench had switched him on again. That the repairs had taken so long revealed how profoundly damaged he had been.

Feeling very pleased with himself, Number Five switched on his laser and proceeded to melt down the rear doors.

Drummond said again, '*HEY*!'

Chigger, seeing the laser in action, decided to sit down again.

'That ain't right, is it?' Drummond said.

'It not only isn't right, it's *impossible*!'

'What do we do?'

'Keep driving!'

Meanwhile, smoke from the melting doors filled the interior of the truck.

Drummond, inspired by some lunacy, reached into his shoulder holster and pulled out an automatic.

Seeing this, Chigger shouted, 'Jesus! Don't let him see a gun!'

At that moment one of the rear doors swung open, and with his route to freedom assured, Number Five turned his attention on his captors. He did indeed see Drummond's gun.

He said, 'Furious, livid, perturbed, angry...'

A neatly aimed shot with the laser beam sent the gun spinning from Drummond's hand in a ball of molten metal.

'Stop, desist, halt, cease,' Number Five ordered.

'Keep driving,' Chigger said grimly. 'On second thoughts, you'd better stop.'

Needless to say, the truck had been lurching and snaking across the road while Drummond's attention had been on Number Five, and at this precise moment the heavy tyres were bumping over the rough ground on the side of the road.

111

'He'll kill us if we stop!' Drummond shouted.

'He'll kill us if we don't!'

Number Five repeated, 'Halt, desist, cease, stop!'

'Okay! okay! I'm stopping!' Drummond slammed on the brakes, and the truck screeched to a lurching, bumping halt. He and Chigger were thrown forward, but Number Five was as steady as a rock. He kept the laser aimed at them.

When the truck had finally settled, he said, as clearly as possible, 'Go, leave, abandon, evacuate, vanish, disappear, depart!'

'That's it, Bimbo!' cried Chigger, and without ceremony kicked open the door on his side and leapt to the ground. Drummond, on his side of the truck, did the same.

Number Five rolled forward to the driving seat.

'Brrrrm!' he said, and eased himself into the driver's seat. With a quick adjustment of the rear-view mirror, he thrust the truck into gear and accelerated away.

He drove hard and fast for five minutes, then turned his attention to the last priority of his emergency repairs.

With his free hand he opened a small panel situated in the side of his body, groped inside, and found the transistorized beacon that always betrayed his position. It was wired into him in such a way that it was supposed to be impossible to remove... but in his new renewed incarnation, such a problem was of minor consequence.

He had it disconnected and removed within seconds. He examined it with interest, it being the one part of his body that, by design, was not integrated into his system.

He transferred it to the hand closest to the window, then reached outside... and whirled his arm so that it span like the blade of an electric fan.

The beacon shot into the distance like a shell fired from a cannon.

Chapter 23

Crosby was wondering idly about a lot of things. For instance, whether to go back and end everything by punching Stonewall on the nose. Whether to go on and end everything (in a different sense) by punching *Marner* on the nose. Whether to try and start something with that girl, Stephanie, call her up some evening and see if she'd like to take in a movie. And whether or not simply to turn the van around and head for Montana.

But most of all he was wondering about Number Five.

E.g., what had made him go wrong. What Stephanie had been trying to tell him about Number Five. How to go about opening up the robot to see what had happened.

He drove along in the field van, ten minutes or so behind Drummond and Chigger, feeling tired, feeling a bit depressed, thinking about all these things. More out of habit than anything else he kept an eye on the orange display of Number Five's tracer.

It glowed with reassuring steadiness. Not at full brightness, because of the distance between the van and the truck, but with such consistency that he was able to judge that both vehicles were travelling at roughly the same speed.

When the tracer began to brighten, Crosby knew that the truck must have stopped. He thought little of this, because his mind was wondering about other things.

A few moments later, the tracer began to dim... indicating, presumably, that the truck had picked up speed again. Once more, he paid little attention to this.

But as the tracer continued to grow dim, Crosby became more interested. Why was the truck suddenly speeding?

And his interest developed into total absorption when the tracer display suddenly showed... Well, according to the orange display, Number Five had abruptly made a 90° degree turn, and hurtled off into the distance as if propelled by a rocket.

Crosby began thinking about this so hard that when he came across Chigger and Drummond, standing disconsolately by the side of the road, he almost drove past them.

Chigger waved him down.

Crosby pulled over to the side, and stared at him through the window. 'You lost him?'

'Any more stupid questions?'

'How *could* you?'

'That's sufficiently stupid. Okay, Cros, he repaired himself. Next question.'

'He did *what*?'

'We put him in a truck full of spares, so he rebuilt himself.'

Crosby just shook his head in disbelief.

'It's impossible,' he said in the end.

Chigger and Drummond climbed up into the cab.

'Want to know something else?' Chigger said.

'What?'

'Well . . . first he did it in about ten, maybe fifteen seconds. Pretty good, that. Second, he hijacked us. That gave us a good laugh, didn't it, Drummond? Third, he drove away in the truck.'

Crosby gaped.

Meanwhile, the tracer beacon was travelling through the air at great speed. Because it was not built for air travel, its lack of aerodynamics quickly slowed it down. Number Five would probably have been disappointed to learn that it only flew for about five miles before coming back to earth. Even then, it did not make it all the way to the ground.

A grocery bag neatly intercepted it, and the tracer beacon came to a halt pressed up between a box of oven-ready pizzas, a pack of Canadian bacon and a carton of Minute Maid Country-Style frozen orange juice.

The grocery bag was in the back of a pick-up truck.
The truck was moving slowly along a country road.

An unexpected problem beset Number Five a few minutes after he threw away the tracer. Although he was driving fast, he had forgotten most of Stephanie's tuition. He was dutifully following white lines whenever he saw them ... but he had forgotten to change gear and was grinding along at sixty miles an hour in bottom.

It was therefore not long before he ran out of gas, and as the truck came to a gentle halt in the middle of the road (its wheels still neatly parallel to the white line) Number Five became genuinely perplexed. He ran exploratory routines throughout the truck's electrical and mechanical systems, but aside from the sticking valve could find nothing wrong.

Just then, a huge eighteen-wheel truck drew up behind him, and blared its horn.

Number Five stuck his arm out of the driver's window and beckoned it on.

The rig did not overtake. A minute or so later, the driver and his buddy walked over to see what was going on.

'Looks like you've run out of gas, friend,' said the driver, before he saw Number Five.

Number Five turned to look at him.

The driver leapt back in alarm.

'Holy shit!' he shouted. 'Lookit that, Bobby! They got damn robots driving trucks now!'

'Oh yeah?' The other man came forward to see.

Number Five acknowledged him.

'Dead, defunct, deceased,' he said, helpfully.

Bobby looked menacing.

'My brother lost his job to a goddam machine,' he snarled.

'You ain't a Teamster!' the driver said. 'Hey, pencil neck! You listening?'

Bobby had gone to the side of the road, and now returned carrying a large rock.

'Let's vandalize his damn ass,' he said, and raised the rock to sling it at the windshield.

'Vandalize,' Number Five said. 'Vandalize, damage, destroy... *disassemble*!'

He lunged into action. With no interest in the men he simply left the driver's seat of the truck by moving forward. He thrust through the dashboard and controls of the truck, burst through the windshield, took half the engine housing with him, and set off up the road leaving a trail of broken glass, bent metal and spinning hub caps.

The driver and his mate were left standing in awe. Bobby put down the rock, feeling very weird indeed.

'You know,' he said. 'Maybe he *was* a Teamster...'

The country road led to the house of Elmer and Beatrice Schmidt. Elmer was driving the pick-up truck along the road and Beatrice was sitting beside him. They had been shopping in town, and their groceries were sitting in two large paper sacks in the back of the truck.

They were looking forward to getting home because their two lovely grandchildren were visiting, and while they had been in town Elmer and Beatrice had bought them a few toys.

Elmer was sixty-eight years old. He had a fine ruddy complexion, and a head of perfectly white hair. He wore a light cotton shirt and golfing trousers. On his head he had a little tweed hat.

Beatrice was sixty-seven. She always wore flowered dresses, and white shoes. Her glasses had gold inlays in the rims, and every week she asked her hairdresser to give her the palest of blue rinses.

They were a nice old couple, Elmer and Beatrice, and as they drove back to their house they looked around happily at the lovely scenery, and congratulated themselves on their choice of a retirement area.

They did not know what had landed in their grocery bag.

Nor did they know that Crosby was wondering where the beacon had gone.

They especially did not know that Stonewall and his troops were busy finding out where the beacon had gone and, unlike Crosby, were doing something about it.

Elmer and Beatrice were therefore extremely surprised to discover that their country road had apparently been invaded by armed troops.

Beatrice's eyesight was none too good, in spite of her gold inlaid glasses, and when she saw the blue uniforms she froze in horror.

'Elmer!' she said sharply. 'You're not going to *stop* for them, are you?'

'They've got guns, Beatrice,' he said mildly.

'Then for God's sake!' she shrieked. '*Hide the dope!*'

But it was not a drugs bust. Not this time.

Later that day came the inquisition. Crosby had taken refuge in his seat at the master terminal in the operations room, but there was no escape from Marner. Nor was there one from Stonewall.

'... Two respectable senior citizens, not a blemish on their lives. It's embarrassing. I'm embarrassed. My troops are embarrassed.'

'Didn't know you had feelings,' Crosby said under his breath, staring at his blank screen.

'Hah!' Stonewall marched over to him. 'You're the wise guy who says this robot's harmless!'

Crosby tried to ignore him.

'Dr. Marner,' he said. 'I know this situation's gotten a little out of hand –'

'Yes, yes, Dr. Crosby,' Marner said, with thin lips. 'At least we agree on *one* point. It has indeed gotten a little out of hand. I hope we also agree on another point. The only thing to do now is destroy Number Five on sight.'

'Yeah yeah!' said Stonewall.

'That's extremely extreme,' Crosby said.

'Oh, is it?' Stonewall asked.

'When you consider that the one thing Number Five hasn't done is harm anyone. I don't know why, frankly, but you have to admit it.'

'You're splitting hairs,' Marner said. 'The thing has become psychotic. The only thing we know about what it's doing is that we *don't* know what it's doing.'

'See?' Crosby said, brightening. 'At least it's consistent in its inconsistency. Just give me some more time. I'm going through the programs line by line. I'll come up with a totally new approach.'

'I've already come up with a totally old approach,' Stonewall said. 'Let Security handle it.'

'Exactly,' Marner said. 'Crosby, you do whatever you can with the computer... and you, Colonel Stonewall, you handle things in the field.'

'Yes *sir*!' said Stonewall. 'Item number one: we bring in the local boys on this. Roadblocks. Lots of them... right across the state, if we need to. Everyone armed, everyone ordered to shoot to kill. We operate night and day. We don't let up until we have the little sonofabitch in a thousand pieces. I want the National Guard on standby, and –'

'– the Air Force ready to nuke him,' Crosby said.

'Right!' Stonewall said. 'No, maybe that's being hasty. But I like your spirit, Dr. Crosby, I like your spirit.'

Crosby stood up.

'One favour, Colonel Stonewall?' he said.

'What's that, kid?' Stonewall was obviously changing his opinion of him.

'Have a heart attack and die.'

Crosby walked out, leaving a room behind him that was full of a sudden silence.

Chapter 24

Stephanie felt tired and numb, as if she had been at a party the night before, and today was the day after. She stood in the shambles of her living-room, realizing that this chaos was the only remaining evidence of Number Five.

It hurt to think about him. If anything, it hurt even more to realize she had played a role – if only an inadvertent one – in bringing him to the fate he feared the most.

Even now his earthly remains would be at the Nova laboratories, while Crosby the Fiend dissected him with electronic knives ...

She made herself a glass of iced tea, and sat down in a half-hearted sort of way on the sofa, wondering where to begin cleaning up the house.

At that moment, Beasley came in from the yard. At least, she thought it was Beasley: a long furry streak went through the living-room at close on a million miles an hour, and vanished out the front. The echo of a plaintive yapping sound hovered in the air behind him.

Moments later the rest of her collection of animals followed, streaming across the floor like the rats of Hamelin.

'Hey guys!' she shouted after them. 'What's up?'

As if in answer, a bush moved slowly into sight, just outside her window. It was a bush she recognized, having planted it herself only three weeks before.

She started to get up.

Then the bush slowly began to rise. From below, pushing it up, came Number Five's head. His eyes appeared to blink.

He said, 'Ste-pha-nie ... ?'

'*Number Five!*' she shouted in delight, and ran out into the yard to greet him. She fell on her knees, and threw her arms around his weird metal body. 'You got away from them!'

'Escape, elude, evade,' said Number Five.

'How did you *do* it? I saw you... you were dead!'

'Repair, recovery, restore.' He patted his shiny new chest with pride.

She hugged him again, then drew back slightly.

'But what are you doing here? If I were you I wouldn't even want to *speak* to me.'

Number Five said, very seriously, 'Stephanie, liar, betrayer, prevaricator, traitor, quisling.'

'Hey, come on! They tricked me, you know that? Tricked, fooled, hoodwinked. I thought you could trust them. I didn't know what they were going to do... honestly!'

'Afraid, man, afraid.'

'Right... and when I get my hands on that Crosby I'm going to –'

'Not Crosby! Crosby, good, innocent, decent, amiable, kind, nice, friend.'

'That louse!'

Number Five rocked emphatically on his tracks.

'Crosby, good, innocent, decent, amiable –'

'You mean that, huh?'

'Yes, agree, confirm.'

'Then who are you afraid of?'

'Man, man, gun, loud voice.'

She stared at him thoughtfully. 'I know who you mean. But look, Number Five, you know you can't stay here, right?'

'Solitude, isolation, alone, lonely.'

'Okay, you can hide out here for a bit. But listen, you never told me you were top secret! Stonewall, the man with the loud voice, he was going to call in the FBI, the CIA, everybody.'

Number Five raised his eye flaps in surprise.

'Alive, Stephanie. Number Five alive.'

'*You* think you're alive... and maybe I do too. But Crosby, he says no way are you alive. He built you... so I don't know what to think any more.'

'Number Five alive,' he said simply.

Stephanie glanced around, knowing that her yard was visible from neighbouring houses.

'You'd better come inside for a bit. But you're going to have to behave. You hear that?'

They went through into the shambles of her living room.

'Ceiling, floor, music, Alan,' Number Five said.

'Yeah ... but you're a walking disaster area. Just look what you did to my place!'

Number Five's head rotated in a full circle.

'Apology,' he said quietly.

'All right, now we've both apologized. But we got to clear this place up. Then we have dinner. I mean, *I'll* have dinner ... you can watch.'

Number Five was proceeding around the room, inspecting the damage he had caused the night before. In the middle of the floor was a heap of magazines. Number Five picked up one from the top, *Better Homes and Gardens*. He read it in a blur of paper, then threw it aside.

'Don't start that again!' Stephanie said.

Without replying, Number Five picked up a candlestick that, the night before, he had thrown on the floor. He placed it on her table, mathematically in dead centre.

He rolled back a couple of inches to admire it.

'Better, improved, ameliorated?' he said.

'All right,' Stephanie said, rather grudgingly. 'But don't break anything else.'

'Observe, watch, see, witness,' Number Five replied, and promptly went into action.

He became a blur, dashing around the room. Stephanie gasped: books went back on the shelves in alphabetical order, magazines were racked in a neat rectangular pile, the carpet was straightened, then vacuumed, the furniture was set upright again, and returned to all the right places, those of her possessions which could be repaired were repaired, those which could not were transferred outside to the trash can,

121

wallpaper was glued back in place, the door was replaced on its hinges, Alan was given exactly the right amount of food, and his oxygen bubbler pipe was cleaned out, the TV was straightened and re-tuned to the channel it had been on before Number Five started watching... and when everything was straight he went around the room and polished everything.

It took about thirty seconds.

As a finishing touch, Number Five dashed outside and repaired the lock on the catering truck's door, then made her a spare set of keys (twenty seconds). He gave her these with a sheepish expression, then pushed her gently into an armchair, and belted into the kitchen.

Before she could gasp, he returned, bearing a plate of food.

'Dinner!' he said proudly, and placed it in her lap.

Dinner was a can of stewed beef, with the lid removed. Number Five had stuck a fork into it, upside down.

Stephanie collapsed into giggles.

Meanwhile, Number Five was attending to the ambience. With great precision he started a record playing, and disco music thundered into the room.

'Excuse, please, allow,' said Number Five, extending his hand.

'You want to *dance*?' Stephanie said incredulously. After the tensions of the day, a dance was something Stephanie could definitely use. She got up, intending to dance around on her own... but to her amazement Number Five insisted on partnering her. He was pretty good too...

Suddenly it clicked: *Saturday Night Fever* had been showing on TV the night before...

It was too much. She danced for a while, but soon she was giggling again.

Then the telephone rang.

It was Stonewall.

'Hallo, Miss Thurber?' he said.

'Yes,' she said, suddenly chilled. She cupped a hand over the receiver, and shouted to Number Five, 'Turn the music down please.'

'Miss Thurber, our little robot seems to have wandered off again. I'd be grateful if you would call me ... you know, if he shows up around there. Call me night or day ... no problem.'

Stephanie said, 'Um, oh ... the robot. Oh, okay.'

Meanwhile, it appeared Number Five had patched things up with Beasley, because the dog had come in from outside, and was licking Number Five's face. The other animals were wandering in curiously to see what was going on.

Number Five called out, 'Stephanie, Stephanie, game!'

She signalled frantically for him to shut up. But Number Five disregarded her. He had started to imitate Beasley's yapping noise, then scuttled around the room sounding like a cat miaowing.

Stonewall said, 'Miss Thurber ... you got someone with you?'

Stephanie shouted, 'Billy, turn down that tv!' To Stonewall she said, 'I'm baby-sitting, you know.'

'Yes, Miss Thurber, I understand *exactly*.'

He hung up on her.

'Forward, Number Five.'

He would not budge.

'Come *on*, will you? We got to get away from here.'

'Hide-out, secure, conceal,' Number Five said.

'You don't understand. We've got to get away from here pronto! It's not safe for you any more.'

'Home, good, warm, happy.'

'Listen to me! That was Nova. You got that? *Nova*! They're coming for you!'

Number Five raced out of the door so fast that he kicked the carpet into mountainous furrows behind him.

Chapter 25

There came a night of feverish activity, none of which was witnessed by Crosby, and none of which led to any result at all. In the morning there was another inquest into what had gone wrong.

Crosby, nursing a hangover, was morbidly pleased that this time it was Stonewall who had done something wrong . . . at least in the eyes of Marner.

'So much for the old approach,' he muttered to Chigger, as they took seats in the operations room.

'Got any ideas of your own?'

'Not really.' He grimaced as pain stabbed the side of his head. 'I've thought of another way of tracing Number Five, but the main problem still remains. What do we do when we find him?'

Marner and Stonewall arrived. From the outset it was obvious that Stonewall was going to bullshit his way out of failure.

'It's espionage, gentlemen!' he said loudly. 'No doubt about it. She's disappeared with eleven million bucks of top secret *materiel*, and she couldn't do that unless she'd planned it all ahead.'

'Espionage?' Chigger said.

'Industrial, political, military . . . take your pick. That's the name of the ballgame.'

Marner had a folder, and he threw this expressively on his desk.

'But she's a nobody,' he said. 'No criminal record, no affiliation to any political party, mainstream or fringe. No college. No communist connections. Born and raised in Masonville . . . the house she lives in used to belong to her parents. They lived there for twenty years. Everyone in that part of town seems to know her. The neighbours think she's unstable... but that's because the house is full of stray animals.'

'She seemed okay to me,' Crosby said quietly, staring at the floor.

'Anything else on her?' Chigger said.

'That's it. And we've got a list of her friends. They're clear too.'

'But what does she *want* with Number Five?' Chigger said.

'Okay, I got it all worked out,' Stonewall said. 'She's broke... we found that out. So she gets Number Five, and sells it. Straight cash deal. Foreign power, hostile political grouping...'

'Maybe make Nova look bad,' said Marner. 'Discredit us.'

'Get on TV?' Chigger said. 'Sell the movie rights?'

Crosby took the file, and started leafing through it with some interest.

'Okay, we got her motives straightened out,' Chigger said. 'Where is she?'

Stonewall bristled.

'We're gonna stake out her house. We got Masonville surrounded. Every highway within fifty miles has police blocks. We've got two choppers searching the desert. Every one of her known regular haunts is being watched. We're staking out the houses of all her friends. The TV stations are running the story. She stole our robot... okay?'

'But you don't know where she is,' Chigger said.

'Goddamn it... no! Not yet!' Stonewall pounded his fist on the desk. 'But it's just a matter of time!'

Crosby closed the file.

'It's all in there,' he said. 'I know exactly what's going on. Number Five's just another stray. She thinks he's alive, and she's rescuing him.'

'You don't know where she is either!' Stonewall shouted.

'No... but I leave all that subtle stuff to you.'

Crosby walked out, and in a moment Chigger followed him.

When Stephanie pulled the catering truck into a filling station for gas, Number Five was watching the portable TV in the back. The Three Stooges were on. Number Five soaked up the input.

Distracted by all the electronic equipment in the filling station, Number Five rolled over to the window to watch. Stephanie went to the office, paid for some gas, then came back to the pump to fill up. As soon as the pump started whirring, Number Five established contact with it, discovered it was in full working order, and watched excitedly.

As the price display approached $10.00, Number Five sent an interrupt to the counting mechanism . . . and the display halted at $9.98. Gas continued to flow.

Stephanie, staring nervously around the filling station forecourt, did not notice.

When Number Five judged that another $10-worth of gas had gone into her tank, he released the interrupt, the price locked into $10.00 and the pump switched off.

When she had replaced the filler cap, Stephanie came and spoke to him.

'Listen, I'm going to make a few phonecalls, okay? Stay out of sight.'

'Yes, agree, confirm.'

Number Five returned to watching The Three Stooges.

Stephanie was gone about ten minutes, and when she returned she had an anxious frown. She got into the driver's seat, and started the engine.

'Worry, alarm, concern?' Number Five said.

'You got it, bozo. I just called six of my friends . . . one of them on the other side of the state line. Stonewall's having them all watched. I was hoping we could go and hide up with one of them.'

'Hide, conceal, camouflage.'

'Right... but it isn't possible. We've got to think of somewhere else.'

She let in the clutch and drove back on to the highway. She had gone no more than a couple of hundred yards when she saw a cluster of police cars ahead, and a line of traffic waiting to get past. Without hesitation she swung the wheel, and did a U-turn. The truck swayed and rocked.

The portable TV skidded down the counter top, and Number Five steadied it with a hand.

'You okay back there?' she called.

'Agree, confirm.'

'Right, well I just thought of where we can go. The one place they'll never think of. Home.'

Chigger caught up with Crosby in the loading bay. He was working feverishly with the backup repair truck, loading it with equipment.

'Hey, what are you doing?'

'I told you... I worked out a different way of tracing Number Five. I've tuned this RF receiver to his operating frequency. It's a long shot, but if I happen to get real close to him, I'll know.'

Chigger peered past him into the truck. There was more equipment jam-packed into it than ever before.

'You've got enough hardware in here to build yourself another robot,' he said.

'This time I'm taking *every* precaution.'

'You know what? You go out there, and Marner's going to fire you. For sure. He's really burned on this one.'

'He said I had to stay at my terminal, right?'

'Right.'

Crosby pointed at a newly installed terminal inside the truck. 'There it is.'

Chigger held out his hand, palm downwards, and pitched it from side to side.

'That's stretching it a bit...'

'I can't just stand by and let Stonewall blow Number Five to pieces. I've *got* to find out what happened. I've got to understand. Understand?'

Chigger stared at him, halfway admiring him, halfway thinking he must be crazy after all. Crosby climbed into the truck, and started the engine.

'You coming?' he said.

'What the hell? I haven't been fired lately. Where do we start?'

He climbed in beside Crosby.

'Well, I don't have much to go on. But a guy at a filling station out on the desert highway called in. He thought she bought some gas there this morning.' He opened a map, folded it back on itself, and spread it out on the dash. 'The filling station's here ... and there was a roadblock *there*. She never got to the roadblock, so I figure she set off into the desert.'

Chigger glanced up at the sun.

'Crazy woman. It's a furnace out there. She could die.'

'I don't intend to let her. Let's go.'

Following Stephanie's strict injunction to stay inside the house and out of sight, Number Five was watching TV in the living room. As they had returned to the house, Stephanie had let out a howl of success ... the whole neighbourhood seemed normal and uninvaded. After three cautious passes of the house she had driven the van into the backyard, parking out of sight behind the trees. She seemed happier at home: the answering machine had been hooked into the phone, the doors and windows were locked ... and she had gone into one of the inner rooms and closed the door.

He had no idea what Stephanie was doing, but his receptor circuits told him she was close at hand, feeling happy. The only thing that puzzled him was a presence of water.

The programme he was watching came to an end, and after

a few commercials – he already knew most of them by heart – there was a newsflash.

Stephanie's photograph appeared on the screen.

Number Five listened and watched with great interest.

He said, 'Ste-pha-nie ... television!'

This so excited him that he entirely forgot Stephanie's instructions to stay in the living room. He trundled off in search of her, following the signals from his receptors.

He pushed open the door. Stephanie was in the bath.

Number Five's eye flaps raised to their fullest extent, and his lenses zoomed forward.

'*Stephanie*, drowning!' he said excitedly.

The moment she saw him, Stephanie made a great splashing movement of limbs, and collapsed backwards in a soapy spray. She went under ... then surfaced, spitting water.

'Hey, bozo, I told you to stay in the other room!'

'Stephanie, save, rescue, release, liberate!' He rolled towards her.

'You stay *right where you are*, buster!' Stephanie said, paddling the bubbly water around to try and cover herself.

Number Five halted uncertainly.

'I'm getting out. You turn your head!'

'Stephanie drown?'

'No, Stephanie not drown. Turn your stupid head!'

With apparent reluctance, Number Five rotated his head until it was facing the other way, but left his receptor pointing in her direction, just in case.

Stephanie scrambled out, hastily towelled herself down, then pulled on her robe.

Rubbing a towel against her hair, she said, 'Listen, Number Five, when I tell you to stay in the living room, I mean it!'

'Head, rotate, turn, circle?' Number Five said.

'Yeah, I guess so ...'

Looking at her he said, 'Stephanie, TV, Number Five.'

'What?'

He returned to the living room, making sure she was following.

When they were both inside, he played her a recording of the newsflash, for good measure projecting the pictures on the screen of the TV set.

He said, in perfect replication of the TV announcer's voice, 'Local woman Stephanie Thurber, of Masonville, was on the run early today after apparently stealing a top security military device from the Nova Corporation. A statewide security net has been laid down for her, and all highways have been roadblocked. Police say that Thurber is armed and dangerous, and if she is seen she should not be approached. More on this story later.'

Stephanie stared at this aghast.

'"Armed and dangerous"!' she said. 'They mean *me*?'

Number Five switched off his recording.

'Number Five, dangerous, deadly, menacing,' he said, looking innocuous.

'They mean the laser, right?'

'Agree, confirm.'

'Well, what this all means is . . . we're in trouble. What are we going to do?'

'Number Five no disassemble.'

'We agree. No disassemble. But we've got to be even more careful now! I don't even know *how* to be careful. I've never done that before.'

She rubbed her hand absent-mindedly against her damp hair. A movement caught her eye, and she turned. Something bright and red was approaching the house. She pressed her face against the window.

'*Oh no*!' she cried. 'That's all we need!'

Chapter 26

'Hi, Steph,' said Frank, getting out of his car. 'I thought I'd find you here. The one place no one would ever think of looking, right?'

'What the hell are you doing here, creep?' She had stepped down from the house, and was marching aggressively towards him.

He crossed to her quickly, and grabbed her arm. Stephanie tried to squirm away, but he held her more firmly, and with his free hand patted her backside.

'Mmm... feels as good as ever,' he said. 'I'd hate to see that pretty little ass wind up in jail. But for ten thousand bucks...'

'*What*?'

'You're a TV star, Steph. There's a fat reward out for whatever it was you stole. What was it, anyhow?'

'None of your damned business!'

'I just couldn't believe it. Stealing secret stuff! You used to get mad at me if I even stole a six-pack!'

'I never stole anything... they're lying!'

She tried to get him to release her, striking at him with her fists, but Frank had always been stronger than her. He started tweaking at the ties of her robe.

'But before I turn you in, hon, we're gonna have some fun, you and me.'

To her horror, he began dragging her towards the thick bushes at the back of the house.

'Don't you dare *touch* me!'

'Just once... for old times' sake.'

As they struggled, Number Five appeared at the door of the house.

'Stephanie,' he said. 'Aid, help, comfort, reassurance?'

131

Frank quit trying to drag her, and stared in amazement at Number Five. But he did not release Stephanie.

'Je-*sus*!' he said. 'Will you look at that! No wonder they're paying so much money!'

Stephanie tried again to twist away from him.

'Forget it, Frank!' she shouted. 'You aren't going anywhere with either of us!'

'Listen to me, Stephanie! I took a lot of crap from you before, but this is *big* money we're talking about...'

'Okay, okay... but he's a computer. You have to talk computer to him, or he won't understand. Tell him exactly what you're doing, where you're going and what you want him to do. Or he won't understand.'

Frank dragged her across to Number Five.

'All right, robot,' he said. 'I want you to come with me. We'll go for a little ride in my car and I'll take you home.'

'Home,' said Number Five. 'Home, secure, safe.'

'What's he talking about?' Frank said to Stephanie.

'I told you... tell him *exactly* where you want to take him.'

'Okay, robot. We're gonna take you home to... Nova.'

A cloud of dirt flew up and gritted into Frank's eyes. When he could see again, Number Five was nowhere in sight.

'You're so goddamn *stupid*!' Stephanie shouted. She managed to get a punch on his face and, as he momentarily slackened his hold on her, she wriggled free.

She sprinted off towards the house.

Frank ran behind her. He caught her up easily, and twisted her arm painfully behind her.

'I'll show you how goddamn stupid I am,' he said. '*You're* still worth ten grand. Let's go.' He began dragging her back around the house, while Stephanie divided her attention between trying to break away from him again, and finding Number Five. He was her only hope... but he seemed to have completely vanished.

They returned to the front of the house where Frank had left his car, to find...

The car had been dismantled. Not broken up, not damaged in any way.

Every screw, rivet and bolt had been undone, and all the parts had been laid neatly on the ground, like the bones of some hapless animal dissected in a laboratory.

Number Five was standing beside it, casually reading through the operating manual.

Stephanie burst out laughing, as Frank at last released her.

'Number Five... that's *wonderful*!' she howled, and doubled up laughing.

Frank stood there in total disbelief.

'He did *that*?'

'Wasn't me,' Stephanie said, and started giggling again.

'I'll blow its goddamn head off!' White with anger, he pulled a gun from inside his shirt, levelled it at Number Five and pulled the trigger.

BLAM!

In one smooth movement, Number Five tossed aside the operating manual, picked up a brake disk, and raised it in front of his face. The bullet struck it, and ricochetted into space.

Number Five said, in the voice of John Wayne, 'Say, Pilgrim, that like to parted my hair. You know, if you want to play rough I can sure oblige you.'

Frank fired again, then again. Both times the bullet was deftly deflected.

'How can he *do* that?' He pulled the trigger repeatedly until the gun was empty.

'Stephanie,' Number Five said. 'Gun, safe, empty, evacuated?'

'It is now.'

Number Five threw aside the disk brake ... but he didn't just toss it casually. He *spun* it, like a frisbee ... straight at one of the pine trees that grew beside the house.

It cut through one of the thickest branches, which fell promptly to the ground.

Frank's jaw gaped. Then he ducked down, grabbed a piston from the remains of his car and hurled it at Number Five. The robot caught it casually, and tossed it aside.

Not to be beaten, Frank then picked up a length of exhaust pipe, and holding it like a lance advanced on Number Five.

He swung it viciously at the robot, who parried it with one of his arms. Frank swung it again and again, exhausting himself, and each time Number Five shrugged it aside casually.

'Stephanie, game!' Number Five called.

'He's trying to *hurt* you!' she shouted. 'Be careful.'

Tiring of the game, Number Five flipped the length of pipe out of Frank's hands, then pushed the young man backwards. He staggered helplessly, and fell backwards into one of the car's bucket seats.

'Smart guy, eh?' Number Five said, in the voice of Edward G. Robinson. 'Who do you think you're pushing around?'

'How smart *is* this thing?' Frank shouted, trying to get out of the seat and keep an eye on Number Five at the same time.

Now it was George Raft's turn to speak. 'Frankie, you broke the unwritten law. You ratted on your friends. When you do that, Frankie, your enemies don't respect you, and you got no friends no more. You got nobody, Frankie.' As he spoke the lines, Number Five picked up a hub cap and flipped it up and down, like a huge coin. Then he said to Stephanie, 'Words, phrases ... correct?'

'You tell him, Number Five!' she said.

But Frank was on his feet again. While Number Five's attention was apparently wandering, he grabbed at the heavy drive shaft of the car, and hefted it like a baseball bat. He dived at Number Five very fast indeed, and brought the immense shaft down on the robot's head.

Number Five keeled over.

Panting, Frank said, 'How about *that*, you goddamn freak!'

He raised the drive shaft for one more crushing blow, but now Stephanie dived to the rescue. She hurled herself against him, sufficiently hard to dislodge his balance.

The drive shaft thudded harmlessly into the ground next to Number Five's head.

With Number Five apparently out of the game, Frank turned his attentions once more on Stephanie. He began hitting her, very hard indeed, and within seconds she fell to the ground. He started kicking at her...

Number Five said, 'No! Not disassemble Stephanie!'

Frank turned in horror.

Number Five was upright again, and his laser was ready for action!

Frank grabbed at the drive shaft, managed to get a hold on it, and raise it...

Number Five fired a burst from the laser. The drive shaft was sliced like salami, *snick, snick, snick!*

Frank threw the remains of it aside, before the deadly beam reached his hands. He started to back away from Number Five.

But the robot wanted to finish him off. He aimed his laser with great precision, and got to work.

Snick! The heels of Frank's cowboy boots were shot away... the man staggered back.

Snick! His beard and moustache were vapourized!

Snick! The belt on his trousers snapped in half!

Sniiiiiick! The metal zip fastener on his trousers burst apart, and his pants fell down! Frank tripped, and collapsed backwards. He covered his head with his arms, and curled up in a foetal ball.

Stephanie went over, and stood so her shadow fell across him.

• 'You want me to tell him to quit playing with you, Frank? Want to see what he does when he's serious?'

'Leave me alone!'

'No... we want you to leave *us* alone.'

'Get lost!'

'Okay... you asked for it,' she said. 'Number Five –'

Frank screamed.

'Don't! I won't ever come near you again, Stephanie!'

'Do you swear?'

'I swear it!'

'All right. Never forget what you're messing with.'

She grinned at Number Five (who had already stowed the laser away), and beckoned with her head. The robot rolled into the back of the catering truck.

'This time, don't move!' she said.

She darted into the house, changed into shorts and a halter top, then hurried back to the van. She got the engine going, and reversed down the drive.

Frank was still lying in a ball, gibbering to himself.

With a snort of contempt, Stephanie accelerated away, heading towards the east. There lay the Oregon desert... the one place there would be no roadblocks.

Chapter 27

The sun was sweltering down, and even with Number Five's air conditioner supplementing the one in the truck it was getting progressively more unpleasant by the minute.

The only relief was the thought of evening . . . but that had a snag too. Desert nights were *cold*, and Stephanie's only clothes were her skimpy halter and pants.

The terrain was worsening too. So far they had avoided getting stuck in the sand, but the ground here was looser, more windblown than it had been when they were closer to the road.

Stephanie was feeling depressed; she was a fugitive with nowhere to go.

Then Number Five said, 'Stop.'

'Stop?'

'Stop, halt, desist, cease, discontinue.'

Having learnt not to question his decisions, Stephanie obediently brought the truck to a standstill.

'Yeah?' she said.

'Strategy. Non-existent, nothing, nowhere.'

'That what you think? Well, maybe you're right.'

'Hide Number Five. Difficult.'

'You don't exactly blend with the wallpaper, I'll give you that. You know, I keep thinking, if we could just get to some expert, some computer genius. Somebody who could make those bozos listen.'

'Not bozos,' Number Five said. 'Bozo.'

'What?'

'One bozo.'

'Who bozo?' She was beginning to think and talk like him . . .

'Bozo: Newton Crosby Ph.D., employee, Nova.'

'You're malfunctioning, pal! He's the enemy.'

'Bozo nice, agreeable, friendly, amiable, cheerful, congenial, pleasant –'

'You think so, huh?'

In another part of the desert, the Nova backup repair truck had also come to a halt. Crosby was deep in thought.

'Listen, I've got another angle,' he said. 'We might be able to bounce a signal off his magnesium casing.'

'Let's get serious, Cros. How many square miles have we covered today?'

'A hell of a lot ... three or four.'

'Great,' Chigger said. 'Only thirty thousand more to go. Let's go back to the road, find a motel for the night.'

Crosby climbed down, and stood outside the truck. The air was cooling at last, as the sun went down, and he took several deep breaths, looking at the radiant sky. Chigger came to join him.

'We could stay out here tonight,' Crosby said. 'You know, build a fire, cook some weenies.'

'You brought some with you?'

'No ... but you know, it's a great idea.'

'Like all your others.'

Crosby kicked at a loose rock.

'Do you think it's this quiet in Montana?' he said.

Chigger regarded him thoughtfully.

'I don't think you're ever going to find out,' he said.

Behind them in the cab the radio suddenly crackled loudly.

Chigger leapt to answer it.

'Yeah?'

'This is Marner. Is that you, Chigger?'

'Yes, sir.'

'Well, I got something for you to tell Crosby. I was just relishing the idea of removing his name from the payroll, but unfortunately I think he might still be useful to me. Is he there?'

'I'm here, Howard,' Crosby said, grabbing the microphone.

'Crosby, I got a call from our unstable friend, Stephanie Thurber. She wants to meet with you.'

'Is this a gag, Howard?'

'Most certainly it is not. God knows why, but she wants to meet with you, and only you.'

'Great!' Crosby said. 'I'll be there! I can handle it. Where does she want to meet, what's the deal?'

Chapter 28

The bar was on a country road, miles from anywhere, the only building in sight. A blue neon sign flashed the words **DINER** and **BAR** alternately, but aside from these there were no outward signs of life. There were a few cars and a pick-up truck in the parking lot, but they all looked as if they had been there for years.

At eight-thirty precisely, a jeep with the Nova insignia painted on the door and hood pulled into the lot, and Crosby got out. He stood in the cool evening air, hands on hips, staring around. It was utterly silent.

A few minutes later he heard an engine, and soon Stephanie's catering truck came along the road and pulled into the lot.

She climbed out, smiling. She held out her hand, and Crosby shook it.

'Uh, hi . . .' he said. 'Is Number Five –?'

'No, he's a long way away. Hidden. He's scared of you guys, you know.'

Crosby swallowed his standard lecture about machines having no emotions.

'Afraid?' he said.

'Well, sure! Wouldn't you be?'

He shook his head. 'I really don't know any more.'

'Why don't we go in? I'm thirsty.'

'Been out in the desert all day?'

'Yes.'

She led the way in. The bar was poorly lit, and the air conditioner was noisy, but there were plenty of places. The bartender was sitting on a stool behind the bar, reading a newspaper.

'I used to come here with my ex-boyfriend,' Stephanie said. 'You like it?'

'No.'

'Neither do I ... but it's useful.'

They sat down in a booth, and after a moment the bartender came over.

'Two beers?' he said, and walked away.

'Gee, I don't know,' Crosby said. 'What are you having?'

'Beer would be okay for me.'

Just then the bartender returned and dropped two cans of beer, wet with condensation, on the table in front of them.

'Two beers,' he said. 'All I got is beers.'

When the bartender was back behind the bar, Stephanie leaned forward on her elbows.

'Let's get this straight from the beginning,' she said. 'Number Five is alive. I don't know how it happened, and he doesn't know how it happened ... but since you built him he's changed. He's *alive* ... like you and me. Get that? It's simple.'

'Okay ... I think we're beginning to realize that now. All I want to do is verify it.'

'Keep at it! You guys act like you're chasing a runaway vacuum cleaner.'

'Okay, I'm sorry. I don't make decisions back at Nova, so I'm not responsible for everything that's been happening.' He took a long sip of his beer. 'But remember this: I built that vacuum cleaner. It's an extremely advanced, extremely complex computerized robot. What I've been saying all along is that it's easy for someone who hasn't worked with computers to interpret its actions as, well, lifelike.'

Stephanie stared at him.

'Dr. Crosby ... we're not going to get anywhere here if you have a closed mind.'

With time to kill, Number Five was seeking more input. Before Stephanie left he had found an old guidebook to the desert in the truck, and now he was out learning botany in the field. A number of wild flowers were growing amid a large outcrop of rocks, and Number Five moved from one to the next, identifying them from the book.

'Coreopsis.' He riffled through the pages in a blur. '*Coreopsis Bigelovii*.' He moved to the next. 'Desert Dandelion ... *Malacothrix Californica* ...'

He moved to another rock. Here something grew straight and tall, a thin wire.

Number Five sent out a receptor call at once, on his guard.

A head, like his own, rose into sight.

It was Number One!

Number Five backed away at high speed, fighting down all instincts to embrace his brother. The input from the receptor call had come like a chill shock of recognition: the icy intelligence, the electronic freeze ... for an instant he had been reminded of himself. Before –

A laser beam sliced through the air, and tore a chunk of rock from the wall above his head. Number Five went on Elude Mode, keeping his physical profile low, boosting his ionization layer to full, muting all electronic output, blocking off all receptor calls.

As he emerged from the rocks, he went on to maximum velocity, but just as instantly cancelled it.

Numbers Two and Three were waiting for him!

Two new arrays of laser beams flashed at him, one glancing off his chest, deflected only by the intense layer of ionization.

Number Five retreated. He had the advantage of thoroughly exploring the rocks earlier, and he had instinctively registered a natural defensive position. He clambered up to it, while the laser beams of his erstwhile brothers tore chunks out of the rocks.

The pursuit of battle had revived his own tactical talents. He settled into his position, then raised his laser, ready to fight to the death.

He saw Number Two scuttling across the desert, trying to find a position from which he could attack. Number Five drew a bead on Number Two, and prepared to fire.

Something stayed his hand. Number Two was a sitting target... his enemies would be reduced from three to two! But he could not fire.

'No!' Number Five croaked. 'Not... disassemble!'

Number One flashed into view, laser aimed. Again, Number Five could have destroyed it. 'No disassemble!' Number Five said again. He retracted the laser, locked it away. He could not bring himself to use it, even in self-defence.

There was no alternative.

Number Five ran checking routines against all his defensive programs... then made a dash for safety. He clambered down the rocks, hit the desert floor, and hurtled away, dodging and weaving.

The desert flowers erupted into flame as he passed. The sand turned to glass. The air was alive with laser beams.

Number Five ran and ran...

Stephanie and Crosby were into their second beers.

'You know he reads books?' Stephanie said.

'He has optical character scanning capabilities, yes.'

'He *reads* them. He understands them, he learns from them.'

'That's what he's programmed to do.'

'Did you program him to dance like John Travolta?'

Crosby looked at her in surprise. 'No.'

'He learnt that from watching TV.' She drained her can of beer. 'He beat me at cards this afternoon.'

'What were you playing... Snap? He's good at Snap.'

'We were playing poker. He learnt it from me. He cleaned me out.'

Crosby gaped.

At last the bar came into sight, and Number Five raced along the road towards it. The three S.A.I.N.T. robots were hard

143

behind him, still squirting their deadly beams of light. Number Five felt more phlegmatic about this, though. Even while the chase was still on he had sent undetected disruptor signals to the aiming mechanism of each of the laser weapons, so that the beams would miss him. He purposely introduced only a narrow error into each one, so that the robots would not realize what he had done and re-adjust the mechanism themselves.

The result was that the shots missed him with plausible narrowness, and he was free to concentrate on high speed, without wasting energy on evasive tactics.

He had therefore gained considerably on his opponents. Only Number One had managed to keep up with him, and was about a hundred yards behind.

Approaching the bar, Number Five sent forward the usual receptor calls and learnt everything he needed to know about the layout of the place. He knew exactly where Stephanie was sitting, and Crosby too.

Number Five veered away from the main building and headed towards an old outhouse. This must at one time have been used as an outside toilet, because his receptor calls turned up a significant stench of rotting material.

Interested by this, and with an idea formed in his mind, he accelerated towards it. Number One followed eagerly.

A few yards from the outhouse, Number Five started ducking and weaving; behind him, Number One began tactical swerves to keep what it imagined was a steady aim.

Number Five slowed, and Number One almost caught up with him.

At the very last instant, Number Five dodged to one side, and jammed on his brakes.

Number One continued straight on, sparks flashing from his tracks as he too tried to halt.

Too late! Number One skidded into the outhouse, demolished the wall... and went head first into the septic tank beneath.

Crosby said, 'Have you actually *thought* about what you're doing? You can't stay on the run forever. And if you could, how are you going to hide something like Number Five?'

'I've thought about it all. I just want to help him.'

'If that's really what you want to do, then let me have him back. He's malfunctioning... he needs to be repaired.'

'Is life a malfunction?' Stephanie said.

'In a robot, yes.'

'So you agree he's alive?' she said with great cunning.

'I didn't mean that! What I mean is, if Number Five has taken on the *appearance* of life, then that's a malfunction.'

'But life itself... feelings, emotions. Never mind Number Five for a moment. Is life itself a malfunction?'

'Obviously not.'

'Life is sacred?'

'Above all else.'

'Then if Number Five *is* alive, you would treat his life as sacred?'

'Yes,' Crosby said.

Numbers Two, Three and Four arrived in hot pursuit, as Number One tried to claw his way unsuccessfully from the septic tank.

Number Five, realizing that at close range the others' lasers would calibrate themselves, knew it was time for a new strategy.

He retreated once more, this time into the parking lot, and took up a defensive position behind the oldest of the cars.

All three S.A.I.N.T. robots were advancing. Number Two approached from the front; the others moved to the flanks.

Laser beams started to punch and fracture the metal body of the car.

Number Five was squatting on a heap of broken rocks and concrete, making his footing insecure. If he needed to retreat again the looseness of the ground would be against him. He ran his tactical program, checked it sixty-three times, and felt alarmed.

It looked dangerous. He was now psychologically incapable of harming the enemy robots, so his laser was effectively useless. All he had left was intelligence ... the only remaining advantage.

Two laser beams stung the side of his head, but the ionization layer deflected them. It was close, though: if he took a beam full on, it would destroy him.

It was time to act.

Number Five reached down and picked up a rock. Then he picked up another. Then a third. He spun his three arms simultaneously: three blurring fans of high-grade duralumin and magnesium.

He released the rocks.

They flew through the air with deadly accuracy. Number Two, Number Three, Number Four ...

Click, click, click! And the recessed buttons on their chests were shut off!

All three of his adversaries froze into immobility.

Crosby was pacing about the bar, while Stephanie sat at the table watching him.

'How the hell *can* I explain it?' he said. 'You won't even let me see him!'

'I've learnt how you guys operate. You and the others get your hands on him ... and the first thing that happens is I go to jail, and the second thing that happens is you start disassembling Number Five.'

'Why won't you listen?'

'I know how you scientists work ... you cut things up to see what makes them go! You'd even do it to animals if you could! Why, I bet you do experiments on monkeys!'

He gestured with exasperation.

'I've never even *met* a monkey!' he said.

*

146

Number Five gathered in the three s.a.i.n.t. robots, and got to work on them. Working in the shadows behind the bar he removed their access panels, and started reprogramming them.

He heard a noise: a crunching of boots on stones, the metallic click of a rifle.

He turned.

Stonewall and his troops were advancing...

Crosby returned to the table, and sat down.

'Okay, Stephanie,' he said. 'What do you *want*?'

'I want it in writing. Signed by everybody at Nova. You will *not* experiment on him. You will *not* flip his switches. You will *not* take him apart.'

Crosby shook his head.

'I can tell you right now. Nova will never go for that. He's still their property.'

'All right,' Stephanie said. 'I'm walking.' She got up to leave.

'You bluffing?' Crosby said.

'No... there's nothing more to say.'

'Just wait a minute.' Crosby took a deep breath. 'Let me tell you... I don't like these guys any more than you do. I don't care if they never get Number Five back. But *I* want to see him ... I have to. I'll do anything you want. Blindfold me, tie me up. I swear I won't do anything to harm him.'

'You mean that?'

'You can trust me, Stephanie.'

He reached out across the table to take her hand, to squeeze it, signifying sincerity, but ... at that precise moment the rear wall of the bar burst apart!

Number Five came crashing through!

'*Stephanie! Stephanie!* A trap, net, delusion! Nova! Hurry! Run, depart, flee!'

She turned to Crosby.

'You *bastard*! You... you... bastard!' She turned to run.

'Wait!' Crosby shouted. 'I didn't know!'

Number Five rushed out of the bar the way he had come, and Stephanie followed.

The bartender put down his newspaper to see what was going on.

Chapter 29

As Stephanie and Number Five scrambled into the catering truck, Crosby rushed up behind them.

'Wait!' he shouted. 'I had nothing to do with this!'

Stonewall's troops had their rifles ready, only holding their fire because they could not get a clear line with Stephanie and Crosby there. Stephanie gave Crosby a look of sheer contempt, then floored the gas pedal.

The catering truck wheeled around, and lurched back on to the road.

'Are you okay, Number Five?' she shouted.

'Agree, confirm.'

She looked in the rear view mirror, and saw Crosby sprinting towards his jeep.

'He's going to follow us!' she shouted.

Number Five moved to the rear of the truck, and pushed the door open. Balanced on the step he watched as Crosby turned out on to the road, and started after them. He raised his laser... He took careful aim...

Red light lanced through the jeep, like a hot knife through butter.

The jeep separated, and the rear end of it careered away. The front, containing Crosby, skidded and lurched, and turned around in a cloud of dust. Then Stonewall, who had followed Crosby in his own jeep, slammed into the wreckage.

But the chase was on! The troops had their own vehicles, and clear orders from Stonewall. Veering around the two entangled jeeps they set off up the road after Stephanie's catering truck.

Number Five, standing at the back, said, 'Stephanie, slow, decelerate, proceed with caution.'

'We got to get away from them!'

'Stephanie, go slow!'

'You know what you're doing?'

'Agree.'

'Okay, bozo ... I hope you do.'

She obediently slackened her foot on the pedal, and the truck slowed down.

And the pursuing trucks started to gain on them...

Number Five waited, not for sake of accuracy, but because he wished to run a counting program of the number of people in pursuit. Input was crucial to him; he still thought in numbers.

Then, when he was ready, he got to work with his laser.

It took three point seven two milliseconds to convert every tyre of every pursuing truck to molten rubber.

A lot of useless trucks littered the road behind them, as Number Five and Stephanie sped away.

Crosby and Stonewall climbed out of their tangled wreckage very slowly, very carefully. No bones broken, just a few bruises, much dust and muck.

Crosby's first instinct was to walk away, to head off into the distance and have nothing more to do with any of this. But Stonewall was there, and Stonewall had betrayed everything. It was a deal Marner had worked out. Crosby would meet the girl alone; no one would try to interfere. A deal was a deal... and Marner and Stonewall, especially Stonewall, had broken it.

Rage coursed through him.

The former soldier was looking up the road at the scattered remains of his troops' convoy. For once he looked crestfallen.

Crosby strode up to him.

'Listen, you stupid sonofabitch!' he shouted. 'You set me up!'

'And you messed it up, *civilian*.'

'Why can't you just keep out of this, Stonewall? I'm sick to death of you screwing everything up!' The memory of

Stepahnie's contemptuous expression was firing him with this bravura display.

'We had it all worked out,' Stonewall said. Some of his troops were walking back, gathering around. 'You distract the girl, and we move in and get the robot with the other s.a.i.n.t. robots.' He wheeled around, suddenly remembering. 'Hey, where in the hell *are* those robots?'

'We lost track of them, sir,' one of the security men said, backing away nervously.

'You *lost track of them*...?' Stonewall said, starting to bristle again. 'You mean now we got *FOUR* lost robots...?' The colonel gestured impatiently, and turned away in despair.

Then Crosby said, *'Look!'*

Everyone turned.

The three s.a.i.n.t. robots were emerging from behind the damaged bar. They were moving in a strange way, jostling and pushing, shouting. They seemed shorter, fatter... One of them had a mop of black hair combed forward. Another carried a short plank of wood over his shoulder, and swivelled it to and fro as he moved so that he kept hitting the others on the head.

As they approached the men could hear what they were saying.

'Oooh! Wise guy, huh!' Number Four poked Number Two in the eye.

'I'll wise guy you, knucklehead!' Number Two punched Number Four on the nose.

Number Three hit both of them with his plank.

'Hey!' shouted Number Four. 'Watch it!'

'Watch this!' said Number Two, and kicked Number Three's backside.

Everyone gaped.

They were Curly, Larry and Moe to the life. Number Five had reprogrammed them to imitate The Three Stooges...

Crosby stared with the others, and then realized what he had to do. But he needed Chigger with him...

Chapter 30

Stephanie struck out into the desert again, knowing its vastness provided the only real safety. She drove and drove, like a woman possessed, until she found a shallow canyon and then she took the catering truck as far inside as she could.

Reasonably sure that they would not be found, she switched off the engine. She was more angry, tense and violent than she had ever been in her life before.

'He set us up! That creep Crosby set us up! I should have known it! It doesn't matter what I say... they've already made up their minds.' She picked up the baseball bat and slammed it on the passenger seat beside her. 'Well, the next time they mess with us, we're gonna kick ass!'

Number Five had crept up behind her, and he canted his head around to face her.

'Kick ass?' he said. 'Donkey, mule, burro...?'

'Listen, Number Five. If they come near you, you *blast 'em*! Fry their asses!'

'Fry?'

'Yeah. Fry 'em! You got a right to defend yourself!'

Number Five's eye flaps furrowed in a frown.

'No,' he said. 'No disassemble.'

'Oh, come on! They deserve it!' It was all too much. Suddenly Stephanie was crying as the tension started to drain out of her. She sat upright, facing straight ahead, eyes closed ... but tears trickled down her cheeks.

Number Five saw this, and peered more closely. He extended a delicate finger and touched her cheek tenderly, running an analysis.

'Salty solution secreted by the lachrymal glands,' he said helpfully. Then he touched his own cheeks to see if he was crying too.

'Oh, no!' Stephanie said. 'What am I talking about?' She tried ineffectually to wipe away the tears. 'I'm sorry... I don't want anyone hurt. I just don't know what to do.'

She got up, and moved into the back of the truck. She pulled a blanket from under the counter, and wrapped it around herself.

'I don't know where to take you,' she said miserably. 'I don't know how to get help, I don't know where to go! I can't even be your bodyguard. You made friends with the wrong person... I'm sorry.' She lay down on the floor of the truck and curled up in a defensive huddle.

Her body shook with grief for a long time, while Number Five watched uncomprehendingly. At last, she quietened, and as her breathing steadied Number Five realized she had moved into that mysterious state called sleep.

He stood there for a long time, standing over her, guarding her, wondering what to do.

Chapter 31

Crosby and Chigger had been searching most of the day, but by sundown even Crosby's zeal had diminished. They had halted the mobile repair truck somewhere in the desert, and fallen into sullen silence.

Crosby was at the terminal, checking, rechecking and re-rechecking the S.A.I.N.T. programs, looking for the elusive clue he still felt certain was there somewhere. Chigger was at the back of the truck, legs stretched out across the floor as he ate some sandwiches.

Breaking the silence at last, Chigger said, 'Want a bite? Real mayonnaise ... no bottled stuff.'

Crosby reached over absently and took one of the sandwiches.

'You know what?' he said. 'I deserve this.'

'It's *my* sandwich you're eating.'

'I mean the whole mess. It's my punishment for selling out to Marner. Fat pay-check every month, all the lab facilities I want ... and no morality.'

'Oh, come *on*!' Chigger said. 'Where else could you play with the kind of hardware we've got at Nova? It's the cutting edge of high technology, man! We've had a lot of fun. You want a pickle?'

Crosby took one with the same distracted air.

'Hermann Goering had a lot of fun,' he said through his sandwich. 'I don't even deserve to eat! Stephanie started to trust me, and now she thinks I'm slug of the month.'

'For God's sake, Cros! She's the one who ripped off the robot.'

'It's not possible.'

'Someone re-programmed him. It *must* be her.'

Crosby washed down his food with a gulp of lemonade

'Okay,' he said. 'Let's take it from the top. Three robots . . . *three* of them. Re-programmed in under ten minutes. Who did it? Wasn't me, wasn't you. Who was it? The girl?'

'What are you getting at?' Chigger said.

'*And* he risked his life to save her.'

'His life?'

'You know what I mean. Those three s.a.i.n.t.s were out to get him, programmed to destruct. Okay, he's surrounded, can fire back . . . but he's in deep trouble. You know what he's programmed to do in those circumtances: "Save your ass, continue mission". Yet he went into that bar to get the girl!'

'He's displaying variant behaviour.'

'Chigger, he's not executing some scrambled version of the original programming. It's *gone*. I don't see any sign of it. Do you?'

'So Stephanie changed it?'

'Sure. First she cracked all the access codes. Then she got hold of the source code from somewhere. *Then* she deciphered that programming language that you and I invented – and you and I are the only two people in the world who know it – and *then* she completely re-programmed him. In an hour or two?'

'So she's some kind of super hacker?'

'Yeah.' Crosby sounded unconvinced. 'And what about the other three? If she did re-program Number Five, by some miracle we can only guess at, how could she re-program *them* without even getting near them? Assuming it would be even possible, which I doubt, assuming that . . . if you and I did it, how long would it take? Ten days? Ten weeks?'

'But what other options are there?'

'By the book . . . none. And by the same book, not even that one. Stephanie *couldn't* have done any of it.' He lapsed into silence.

'Wait a minute,' Chigger said. 'If you're getting at what I think you're getting at, I think you should stop getting at it. I can't handle it. I'm just the apprentice genius . . . okay?'

'I'm running out of scenarios. There's only one left, and I can't handle it either.'

They were interrupted by a sudden *squawk*! It came from a little audio speaker taped temporarily to the wall of the truck. They both moved, and peered at the various instruments they had set up.

'It's the RF receiver,' Chigger said. 'You tuned it to Number Five's wavelength, right?'

'Yeah... but it must be a mistake. We wouldn't get a reading unless he was less than twenty feet away.'

CRASH! The rear door of the truck slammed open, almost torn from its hinges.

It was Number Five.

His eyes glowed with a fierce red light, and his laser was at the ready!

'Hello bozos!' he said.

Crosby and Chigger stood frozen with fear. They both slowly raised their hands.

At that precise moment, Marner decided to call in on the radio and see what they were up to.

'Crosby? I'd like to know where the hell you are, and what the devil –'

SNICK! VOOP! The radio turned into a molten blob.

Number Five turned his laser towards Chigger.

'Ben "Chigger" Thurley. Delete!'

'Hey! Wait a minute...' Chigger looked at Crosby in real alarm.

'Correction,' Number Five said. 'Apology, Ben "Chigger" Thurley. Depart, exit, leave...'

'That's one hell of a mistake to make!' Chigger said in relief. 'Come on, Cros. Let's run for it!'

Chigger pushed past the robot and Crosby tried to follow, but Number Five turned his laser on him fiercely.

'Newton Crosby Ph.D. No run. Drive, propel, steer...'

Chigger was outside, looking back in.

Crosby said, 'I think he wants me to take him somewhere.'

156

'Agree, confirm.'

'But without you.'

'Agree, confirm.'

Chigger shrugged nonchalantly. 'That's okay. It's not far to the road.'

'You sure?'

'Newton Crosby Ph.D.... *drive, propel!*'

'Okay, okay... I'm just saying goodbye to my friend.'

'Friend, buddy, chum, pal, associate,' Number Five said with a backward glance at Chigger. 'Goodbye, farewell, cheerio, au revoir.'

'And you have a nice day yourself,' Chigger said.

Moments later, the repair truck swirled off into the desert.

Chapter 32

It was dark. Where was Number Five? She was alone!

Stephanie woke up, alarmed. Something had made a noise.

Groggily she stood up, listened. Then she heard an engine, the crunch of tyres on sand and stone. She grabbed the baseball bat and went to the window. The repair truck was there, the Nova insignia gleaming insolently on its side.

She saw Crosby climbing down from the cab.

She sprang into action. She leapt out of the back of her truck like a vengeful demon, baseball bat raised, anger spitting from her.

'All right, creep! You're dead! Where's Number Five? What have you done with him?'

Crosby backed away, raising a hand defensively.

'Nothing! Nothing!'

'Come on, bozo! Spill!' Then she saw Number Five, clambering down from the rear of the repair truck. 'You kidnapped him!'

'Kidnap, shanghai, hijack,' said Number Five.

'Look,' said Crosby. 'There's something you have to know. They set me up! I only wanted –'

'Listen horse face! *We*'re not talking! I've nothing to say to you any more!' She gestured wildly with the bat at Number Five. 'Talk with him! Get it into your thick skull that he's alive, intelligent. Then when you've done that, you go tell it to *them*! Okay?'

'Okay . . . then what?'

'Then you tell them to *LEAVE US ALONE*!'

'Stephanie, could you just tell me, calmly, quietly . . . What are you doing? I mean, are you trying to make a name for yourself? Are you in this for the money? Do you just hate weapons research? What?'

'Give it *up*!' Stephanie cried. 'Will you just give up and go talk to him. Go and *talk* to him. Please!'

'I've been trying to communicate with him for four days,' Crosby pointed out.

Number Five reached up and put a hand on Crosby's shoulder.

'Communicate, input, need input! Questions, queries, posers, problems, puzzles...'

'You see?' Stephanie gestured towards a nearby hilltop. 'Look, there's a place up there. It's quiet, no-one's gonna bother you. Sit down, just the two of you. Look at the stars, get to know each other.'

Number Five said, 'Beautiful stars better see.'

Crosby looked at him sharply.

'"Beautiful stars better see"? He means... er, it's easier to... to triangulate his position from up there.'

Stephanie threw aside the baseball bat in exasperation.

'Oh, my God! Are all geniuses as stupid as you? He means it's a beautiful night... the stars are beautiful.'

Crosby stared at her.

'You kidding?'

'You heard him say it. Remarkably articulate, for a four-day-old.'

'Beautiful sky, beautiful stars,' said Number Five. 'See beautiful stars. Come. Come. Need input!' He started rolling towards the hill, and beckoned to Crosby with one of his hands.

Crosby hesitated just a few moments longer. He looked from Stephanie to Number Five, then back again.

'Is it sinking in yet?' Stephanie said.

Number Five was waiting.

'Right!' Crosby said. 'Okay... but just a second!'

He dived into the repair truck, seized a whole bundle of listings, programs and blueprints, as well as a portable lantern, then followed Number Five eagerly up the hill.

159

Chapter 33

They came to a shallow dip in the side of the hill, screened by jagged rocks and with a soft, sandy floor. Number Five gestured with a sweeping motion towards the sky.

'Beautiful, agree?'

'Yes, Number Five. Beautiful.' Crosby shook his head, wondering what he had come to, discussing aesthetics with a crazy robot. 'We got a lot to sort out.'

'No disassemble.'

'That's the deal, yes.' He cleared his throat. 'Okay, let's begin. Number Five. Verbal Command Override. Access code Crosby: four two seven nine one.'

'All command access patches disabled,' Number Five said calmly.

'By whom? Name programmer.'

'Number Five.'

'You did it yourself?'

'Confirm.' Number Five trundled forward, and pulled open his chest panel to reveal the rewiring inside. Holding the lantern, Crosby peered in.

It was a crazy maze of wires, circuit boards, solder joins, silicon chips. The neat solidity of the s.a.i.n.t. processors, which he and Chigger had slaved over for so long, had been replaced by a coloured spaghetti of makeshift circuitry. Nothing was where it should have been.

Then Crosby's heart missed a beat.

There inside, tucked away but still accessible, was Number Five's master switch: a simple toggle, marked ON/OFF.

The presence of the switch dominated every thought. He backed away, playing for time while he worked out his chances of getting to it.

'You said you had questions, Number Five,' he said. 'What do you want to know?'

'Important... most important. Life. *Why?*'

'You mean, why are we alive?' Crosby put down the lantern to have both hands free, then moved back so that he was facing Number Five, the ON/OFF switch just inches away from his hand. 'Well, you know... that's an awfully big question. We're alive, I guess, to do things. Like, invent things, for example. To raise children, and –' With a movement like a snake lunging at a prey, Crosby thrust his hand inside Number Five's chest and hit the ON/OFF switch! '– and to turn off malfunctioning robots!' he finished triumphantly.

Number Five was immobile, frozen in his last position.

'First lesson, bozo... never trust a human. Now let's have a look at what you've been up to...' Crosby leaned forward for a closer look at the wiring, but as he did so two things happened at once. Firstly, the ON/OFF switch turned itself back on... and secondly, Number Five moved one of his powerful metal arms and pushed Crosby aside.

Number Five rolled back a pace or two. His eyes were glowing. When he spoke, his voice came out in a roar:

'NUMBER FIVE ALIVE! LIFE *NOT* MALFUNCTION!'

Crosby flinched away, knowing that Number Five could have crushed him with his arm, had he so chosen. The robot moved to the side, brought one of his arms down on a rock, and with an angry karate chop broke it in half. He turned back to Crosby, who was cowering away.

Number Five said, in his normal voice, 'Apology, Crosby. Anger, rage, fury, petulance, sulk.'

'Okay, okay. I won't try anything again.'

'Can *not* try anything.'

'Yeah, I figure. Tell me, you rewired all the switches too?'

'Switches my switches. Control mine. Master switch test for Crosby. Curiosity: Crosby attempt to disassemble? Result, affirmative.' Number Five waggled his head

161

reprovingly, like a teacher catching a child misbehaving.

'Hell, I'm sorry, Number Five. I didn't understand.'

'Trust?' said Number Five.

'On my honour.' This time Crosby meant it. 'Can I try another approach?'

'Ohjay.'

'*What?*'

'Apology: okay.'

Crosby shook his head, amused.

'Right, you're out there in the desert, and you see a tank approaching. A Soviet T-54 tank. It's coming straight at you, and it's got its gun loaded. What would you do?'

'Run away, hide, telephone police.'

'You're *kidding*! What about your programming?'

'Override programming.'

'Fine ... you get yourself blown up. Command: Disregard override. What is your response?'

'Disregard disregard command. Run away.'

Stephanie appeared at that moment, carrying a big bowl of hot soup and a chunk of brown bread. She gave it to Crosby.

'You're gonna need this.'

'Uh, thanks!' he said.

'How's it going?'

'This guy just breaks me up,' Crosby said. 'I mean –'

'Have fun!' Stephanie squeezed his hand, gave him a little smile, and went away again.

'All right, Number Five,' Crosby said. 'You've learnt how to override your programming. That doesn't mean you're alive.'

'What *does* it mean?' Number Five said.

'Well – you know, it means ...'

Crosby sat down on the sand and thought about it. The soup tasted good.

'Okay,' Crosby said, pacing to and fro. 'Let's agree that you've found a way of overriding the programs. Let's also agree, for the moment, that this might *or might not* mean you're alive. What I want to know is, *why* did you override?'

'Program says destroy. Destroy disassemble. Make dead. Number Five can not. Can *not*.'

'Why cannot?'

'Wrong, incorrect, immoral.' Number Five rolled towards him earnestly. 'Newton Crosby Ph.D. not *know* this? Number Five explain?'

'No thanks ... that's unnecessary. Of course you're right. But who told you?'

'I told me.'

Crosby found a sheet of print-out without too much print on it, and laid it on the ground. Then he poured the dregs of his soup into it, and folded the paper in half. The result, intended to be an impromptu Rorschach Test, was a messy orange smudge.

'Okay, wise guy,' he said to Number Five. 'Analyse.'

Number Five touched the paper, then the smear of soup.

'Wood pulp,' he announced. 'Some cotton content, plus other cellulose fibres.' He moved on to the soup. 'Water, tomato, cornflour, salt, hydrolysed vegetable protein, monosodium glutamate, sugar, artificial flavour, artificial colour.'

'Not true!' Crosby yelled.

'Is true.'

'It can't be. She's a health food freak! She wouldn't have garbage like that in her truck.'

Very seriously, Number Five said, '*Is true*, Crosby. Query, tell Stephanie?'

Crosby regarded the robot with new respect.

'No ... better not.' He waved the sheet of paper again. 'Come on ... and the rest of it! What's it look like to you?'

'Mark look like, resemble ... butterfly, bird, maple leaf.'

Crosby took the paper back, and looked at it from several angles. Number Five was right.

'Holy cow!' he said.

Number Five snatched the paper back, and looked at it again.

'No cow,' he said.

They got down to the serious stuff, and Crosby spread the various plans and blueprints across the sand. Using Number Five's light-source to supplement the flickering lantern, the two of them pored over the plans, going through every inch of the designed circuitry and comparing what should have been with what had now become.

Crosby called out the checklist, and Number Five either confirmed that the relevant part was still as designed, or explained calmly what had been done to modify it.

Crosby noted down all the changes . . . and the picture began to take shape.

'Right, I think I've got this all located,' he said. 'I can pin down your logic boards, your reason circuits, and the overall intelligence simulation. All the motor functions are more or less unchanged. But I can't locate the vocabulary store, and I'm stuck on aesthetics. Most of the rest is easy enough, though.'

Number Five turned his head to look at him.

'You understand me, Crosby?' he said.

'I reckon so.'

'Explain Number Five,' he said, and leant over the plans again, seeming to search for something.

'What do you want explained?' Crosby said confidently.

'Query, location of sense of humour?'

Crosby threw down his pencil, and sat back in an expansive gesture of disbelief.

'Look, Number Five,' he said. 'You got everything you need, right? But there are some things that are going to be permanently beyond you. A sense of humour is one of them.'

'Apology, Crosby,' Number Five said humbly.

Crosby got up to pace about, but he took only one step

before falling flat on his face! Someone had tied his shoelaces together...

Number Five looked away innocently, his metal lips puckered, as if whistling softly.

Later, with his pride starting to recover, Crosby took Number Five through a set of the standard AI routines. He passed each one with honours, treating them as if they were elementary spelling tests...

Crosby taught him how to play Simon Says. Number Five loved it, and on the second round completely tied Crosby in knots...

He tried the Socratic Method of reasoning on Number Five, and (when that failed to reveal the robot as an impostor) moved on to Socratic Irony, to test him for areas of ignorance.

This too was quickly abandoned, when the major areas of ignorance were revealed to be in the inquisitor.

'Okay, smart guy,' Crosby said. 'Go write a novel.'

'Which one?' said Number Five, and proceeded to recite the Maude translation of *War and Peace* until Crosby, driven to distraction, pleaded with him to quit.

'I need to think,' Crosby said, and went away to stand by himself by the jutting rocks. He could see Stephanie's truck on the plain below, and beyond, across the flat sea of sand, the sun was beginning to rise. The sky turned quickly from black to dark blue, then to pale blue tinged with pink clouds.

He was still sore about the shoelaces gag, and all that had followed. The serene beauty of the sunrise started to soothe the fevered breast, in time-honoured fashion, and Crosby put aside feelings of personal slight and thought about the problem objectively.

Number Five passed all the tests. He *acted* as if he were a sentient being. But something still stuck in Crosby's craw. There must be one last test... something that would validate

Number Five's claim that he could *feel*.

But even with his new feeling of objectivity, Crosby still felt irritated by the practical joke that had been played on him.

Then he thought: Number Five can give a joke ... but can he *take* one?

Crosby ran down the hill to Stephanie's truck, and quietly opened the rear door. Stephanie was asleep on the floor, curled up in her blanket. He tiptoed past her, then took one of the stools from behind the counter.

When he was back with Number Five he said, 'I want to test your motor functions, Number Five. Okay by you?'

'Confirm.'

'All right. You seen this before? It's a stool. Humans use it to sit on. I'd like you to try.'

Number Five made a slight shrugging motion.

'Motor functions normal,' he said.

'Yeah, but even so.' Crosby held out the stool. 'Turn around, and lower your backside on to the seat.'

Number Five looked puzzled, but he readily complied.

As his rear torso lowered towards the seat, Crosby whipped it away from underneath him.

Number Five sat down in the sand, looking puzzled.

'Query: why move it?'

'*Ha*, sucker! Fell for it, eh?'

Number Five stood up, then, with some dignity, removed the clinging sand from his lower body.

'Not understand, Crosby. Moral: dangerous activity. Risk spinal injury to humans. Discourage repetition.'

'You don't find it funny, then?'

'Not funny. Is funny?'

'Yeah ... I think so.'

'Try funny,' said Number Five, then added as a precaution, 'Real funny.'

'You want a joke?'

'If funny. Not not.'

166

'All right then.' Crosby stared at him, trying to think of a joke. One came into his mind. 'Try this, then. You ready?'

'Was that joke?'

'I haven't started yet. Okay... There's this man, see, and he goes into a bar. He's already very drunk, and staggering all over the place. You getting this?'

'Understand bar, drunk, staggering. Dangerous activity. Discourage repetition.'

'Yeah, yeah... but this is just a story, right? So he goes into this bar, and he's crashing into the tables and knocking chairs over, but in the end he makes it okay to the bar.'

'You said was in the bar already.'

'Well, see, there's a bar that's a sort of building you go to for a drink, and *inside* that kind of bar there's *another* kind of bar... like a counter.'

Number Five said, 'You explained badly.'

'You're supposed to know the difference.'

'Do now. Input.'

Crosby felt a numbing sense of hopelessness. He hated having to explain jokes... and wished he hadn't started.

'Proceed,' said Number Five. 'Interested, input.'

'No, forget it... this isn't going to work.'

'Proceed!'

'All right. So this man gets to the bar, right? And he calls the bartender over. You know what a bartender is?'

'Confirm.'

'Okay, so he says to the bartender, "I want you to tell me something. How tall is a penguin?"'

'Penguin,' said Number Five. 'Flightless marine bird of the order *Sphenisciformes*. Height usually in the region of thirty to forty inches. Problem solved.'

Crosby looked up at the sky hopelessly.

'Will you *listen*?' he said. 'I'm telling you a joke!'

'Not funny.'

'*I haven't FINISHED yet!*'

'Apology. Proceed.'

Crosby took a deep breath. 'This time I'll tell you when it's over. Okay?'

'Confirm. Proceed.'

'All right. So he says to the bartender, "How tall is a penguin?"... and the bartender says, "I'm not sure but I think they're about *this* big", and he holds his hand about thirty inches from the ground.'

'Correct,' said Number Five. 'Proceed.'

Crosby glared at him.

'So the man says, "You sure?", and all the other customers in the bar confirm it. So the man says, "Aw hell, I think I just drove over a nun"!'

Number Five said, 'Proceed.'

'That's it. It's finished.'

'That is joke?'

'Yes.'

'Not funny.'

'Sure it is. One of the best.'

'None, not one, no one, nobody. Not understand.'

'Not "none", you bonehead! *Nun!*'

Crosby made a private resolution: never, under any circumstances, never *ever* tell a joke to a robot again.

'Nun?' said Number Five.

'Yes.'

Number Five wheeled around and propelled himself to the other side of the little hollow. There he hunched down, appearing to contemplate the ground. Ten seconds passed in silence.

Then Crosby noticed that his frame appeared to be vibrating slightly.

Number Five raised himself to his full height, and turned around. His eyes were red with light.

He said, 'I think I just drove over a nun!' And he started vibrating again, emitting a low electronic whirring noise. It steadily increased in frequency, becoming a modulated whining, broken by a kind of coughing noise. Then it got louder and louder, becoming a deafening cackle. Soon, Crosby had to cover his ears as Number Five's weird, braying laughter rang out across the desert.

Stephanie, woken by the racket, raced up the hill to find out what was going on.

She found Crosby and Number Five leaning on each other, arms around each other's shoulders, intermittently doubling up, howling with laughter, and shouting incomprehensible phrases.

'TELL ME, HOW TALL IS A *PENGUIN*?' shouted Number Five, and screamed with electronic laughter. Crosby staggered away, wheezing and holding his sides. 'I THINK I JUST DROVE OVER A *NUN*!' he yelled, and Number Five fell over backwards, kicking his caterpillar treads in the air.

'Would you guys mind telling me what's going on?' Stephanie said loudly.

Crosby noticed her and staggered over, still giggling, choking it back, trying to keep a straight face.

'I just told the funniest joke of my life,' he said, and turned away, bent over double and pitched forward, rolling with laughter.

Number Five tried to get up, but fell over again.

'Some joke, huh?' Stephanie said.

No answer from either of them, apart from renewed gales of laughter.

'I'm waiting,' Stephanie said, tetchily.

Crosby sobered at last.

'You want to hear the joke?' he said.

'Unless you'd like me to get the baseball bat...'

'Okay.' Crosby repeated the story, punctuating it with muffled snorting noises.

At the end, Stephanie said, 'That's not at *all* funny.'

'*He* thinks it is,' Crosby said, pointing at the prostrate Number Five, who was still giggling helplessly. 'I suppose that's what counts.'

'Then that's that,' Stephanie said. 'It's all over. You agree.'

'Yup.'

'Number Five's alive?'

'No question.'

'All life is sacred?'

'We agreed. A deal is a deal.'

Stephanie let out a great roar of excitement.

'Number Five! *Number Five!*' she shouted. 'You hear that?'

Number Five instantly stopped laughing. He rolled further back, then in one bound jumped forward so that he landed on his feet, like an acrobat.

'I heard,' he said. 'Number Five alive!'

Stephanie threw her arms around Crosby's neck and planted a long, affectionate kiss on his lips. Then she danced over to Number Five, grabbed two of his hands and started to waltz around him. Number Five responded by a quick burst of disco dancing. Crosby watched in amazement.

But suddenly the joy ceased.

There came the sound of a heavy engine, and the clanking of metal treads. The peace of the desert was shattered.

Number Five froze, extending his receptors.

'Tank, American, M-60,' he said. 'Run, hide, *telephone police!*'

Chapter 34

'Let's go!' Crosby shouted, and grabbed Stephanie by the wrist.

She dragged him back.

'What?' she cried. 'We can't keep running forever! Just tell them he's alive!'

'It's not that simple! Come on!'

Number Five was already halfway down the hill. After a moment's hesitation, Stephanie began to hurry after him.

'We had a deal,' she said to Crosby as they ran. 'The plan was: we convince you, and then you convince *them*!'

'They won't necessarily believe me. Look how long it took to convince me ... and I'm *intelligent*!'

'Look how long it took me to notice that.'

She dashed towards her catering truck, but again Crosby snatched at her arm to restrain her.

'We'll go in the Nova truck ... it's faster.'

'Does it make any difference?'

Crosby jerked his thumb back: the tank was nosing over the ridge.

'We can outrun that in it,' he shouted.

Number Five was waiting by the repair truck, and leapt in as Crosby and Stephanie went to the front. By the time they had sat down, Number Five had moved up to the front and was squatting down behind them.

Crosby got the engine going, wheeled the truck around and accelerated away up the shallow canyon.

'Why won't they believe you?' Stephanie said. 'I thought you were the big shot.'

'I'm the eccentric genius. They don't believe half of what I say ... and they don't understand the rest.'

'Then *make* them listen. It's your *duty*!'

'Duty, responsibility, obligation,' said Number Five.

'I think there's one thing you're not quite clear about,' Crosby said. 'They're not going to give up until they're sure he's destroyed. They think he's dangerous.'

'So tell them he's not.'

'What do I say? "Listen, folks, remember that killing machine you built. Turns out it's harmless." They'd never buy that line. Anyway, he's an embarrassment to them. Eleven million dollars of taxpayer's money for a machine that won't do what it's told.'

'This is America! He can do whatever he wants!'

'An American can... they think he's a robot. Worst of all, he's Top Secret... a national security risk. They don't want to see him on the cover of *Popular Science*.'

She stared out of the window. She could just make out the dark shape of the tank in the rear-view mirror; it was already a long way behind them.

'So what do we do?' she said.

'We keep driving.'

'I already tried that. It doesn't work.'

'Well, *I'm* driving now.'

They had reached a level stretch of the desert, with a ridge of rocks rearing up on one side. The ground seemed firm, so Crosby kept building up the speed. Neither of them could see the tank any more.

'Maybe we're gonna make it,' Crosby said.

'Maybe we're not.'

A shadow crossed their path, causing Crosby to swerve, and when he straightened they saw a huge, dark-green military helicopter coming in to land a few hundred yards ahead of them.

'Shall I go around it?' Crosby shouted.

'Go *around* it? Then what? You'd better stop.'

'Giving up, Stephanie?'

'I told you... I've been driving for the last three days. It's hopeless.'

Crosby slammed on the brakes, then appeared to change his mind. He threw the truck into reverse, backed up, then accelerated towards the rocks.

The helicopter simply shifted position, and settled in front of them again.

Trucks had appeared at each side, blocking any hope of retreat.

The repair truck came to a halt in a cloud of dust and sand. As it began to settle, Crosby and Stephanie could see troops running from the trucks, taking up position. They were heavily armed... grenade launchers, anti-tank weapons, rockets. These were no longer Stonewall's private army, but members of the National Guard.

'Jee-suz,' Crosby breathed. 'They mean business this time.'

Number Five said, 'Fear, anguish, dread.'

'You got it, bozo.' Stephanie reached up and patted his head. 'But this time we're all in this together. Don't worry about a thing.'

Marner, Stonewall and Chigger had alighted from the helicopter, and had moved to the cover of one of the trucks. Chigger at least had the grace to look sheepish. Marner was carrying the bullhorn.

'CROSBY... ARE YOU IN THERE?'

Crosby reached across to Stephanie, and squeezed her hand. 'Take it easy... stay calm.' He opened the truck door, and stood up on the step. He shouted to Marner, 'It's okay, Howard... everything's fine. Number Five is here with us, and I've got it completely under control.'

Marner appeared to ignore this.

'STEPHANIE THURBER!' he bellowed. 'YOU ARE ALREADY IN VERY SERIOUS TROUBLE. RELEASE DR. CROSBY AT ONCE.'

'I don't believe this,' Crosby said, getting into the cab again. 'They think you're holding me hostage, for God's sake!'

'Didn't Number Five take you away at the point of a laser?'

'Yes, but that was yesterday.' He thought hard. 'Look, we'll get out together, and show them I'm okay. But stay close to the truck.'

'What about Number Five?'

'He stays in here. Understood, Number Five?'

'Confirm.'

Stephanie said to him, 'Don't worry... we won't leave you.'

Number Five started rocking back and forth.

'Stephanie, run, hide. If disassemble me, disassemble you too!'

'Nothing can happen so long as we all stay close together. They won't try to shoot while we're here. They're not that crazy...'

'I'm not so sure any more,' Crosby said. 'Look, I'll try to talk to Chigger. He'll listen to reason. Come on, let's get this over with.'

Very slowly, very cautiously, they climbed down from the truck. Now they were outside, the encircling troops seemed frighteningly close.

Stephanie stayed right up against the side of the truck, spreading her arms across its wall.

She shouted to the nearest group of soldiers, 'Don't you dare try *anything*!'

'Chigger!' Crosby called. 'You there?'

'Yes, sahib.' He stepped uncertainly from his cover.

'Chigger, look. I'm fine, Stephanie is fine. We just don't want any shooting. Number Five mustn't be damaged.'

Marner drowned everything out.

'DR. CROSBY! YOU AND THE GIRL GET AWAY FROM THAT TRUCK. *WE'LL* TAKE CARE OF NUMBER FIVE!'

From inside the truck came a muffled voice.

'Get away, Stephanie... get away! Danger!'

'It's okay, Number Five. Stay there.'

'Maybe we should show them the robot,' Crosby muttered.

174

'Shouldn't we ask Number Five first?'

'Leave it to me.' Crosby edged his way along to the rear door of the truck, but it wouldn't budge. 'Did you lock the back?' he said to Stephanie.

'No. Number Five must have done it.' She tapped on the side of the truck. 'Number Five ... you okay?'

No answer.

'WHAT THE HELL'S GOING ON, CROSBY? GET AWAY FROM THAT TRUCK, OR WE'LL START SHOOTING ANYWAY!'

'Bullshit!' Crosby shouted.

'Why don't you tell them he's alive?' Stephanie said.

'Because they'll think I'm nuts. I've got to tell them something they'll believe.' He turned towards Marner and the others. 'Listen, Howard! I've rendered Number Five harmless. I was able to activate the Voice Command module.'

Marner, Stonewall and Chigger held a brief consultation, glancing back in their direction. They could see Stonewall shaking his head emphatically.

'DR. CROSBY,' Marner bawled. 'YOU'RE LEAVING ME NO OPTION BUT TO CONSIDER CRIMINAL PROCEEDINGS AGAINST YOU AND THE YOUNG WOMAN.'

Crosby glanced at Stephanie.

'You see how crazy they are?'

'Wouldn't that be better than them shooting at us?'

'Sure ... but they're gonna do that anyway!'

Stonewall was shouting instructions to the men, and two groups dispersed and took up new positions. Metal catches on weapons made a nasty clicking sound. Then Stonewall grabbed the bullhorn from Marner.

'LISTEN GOOD, CROSBY. WE ACCEPT NO RESPONSIBILITY FOR WHAT IS ABOUT TO HAPPEN... UNLESS YOU WALK AWAY FROM THE TRUCK NOW!'

'I'm staying put,' Crosby said. 'What about you?'

Stephanie took his hand.

'We're in this together,' she said.

Unexpectedly, a detachment of men suddenly broke cover and rushed towards the truck. They were unarmed.

'Let's get 'em, Cros!' Stephanie yelled, raising her fists. 'You take half, I'll take the other half!'

'But there's twenty of 'em!'

'Ha!'

But the men were only halfway across the distance before events changed drastically!

The rear doors of the truck burst open!

Number Five crashed to the ground.

'Cheerio, Stephanie!' he said as he hurried past. 'Au revoir, Crosby!'

'What you *doing*!' Stephanie screamed.

'Run, hide, get help!' He rushed away.

Stephanie shouted after him, 'Number Five, *Number Five*... don't run... DON'T RUN!'

But he was already out of earshot. With his head down low, Number Five was hurtling across the desert, kicking up an immense trail of dust behind him. He weaved and dodged.

Troops started firing at him! Number Five's immediate response was to change direction. In a magnificent skidding turn, he turned right around and headed back. He zoomed at top speed towards Marner and Stonewall!

As the troops swivelled their rifles around to follow him, Stonewall yelled in a sudden panic, 'DON'T FIRE! *HOLD YOUR FIRE*!' He and Marner dived in opposite directions.

Number Five scorched through the place they had been standing, then did another spectacular reversal of direction while the troops jostled to get a clear line on him.

Now Number Five was racing along parallel to the ridge of rocks, ducking and swerving once again, and the soldiers turned around, their weapons trained.

'FIRE AT WILL!' Stonewall shouted. 'GET THAT DAMNED THING!' More of the troops left their positions and began to run after Number Five.

'He's deliberately leading them away!' Crosby said. He cupped his hands around his mouth. '*Don't shoot! He's alive, he's alive!*'

'They're going to *get* him!' Stephanie shouted in great panic.

Number Five was making a determined effort to escape. His fast-moving tactics made shooting difficult, especially as he had developed the ploy of running between groups of the soldiers to make it difficult for them to fire. But he was not getting away unscathed: Crosby and Stephanie saw several bullets strike him directly.

'We've got to stop this!' Stephanie said, and broke cover. She ran towards Number Five, right through the field of fire. After a moment, Crosby too left the comparative safety of the truck. He dashed across to Chigger.

'Chigger, we've got to stop this madness!' he yelled. 'Someone's going to get killed!'

'Sorry, Cros ... it's out of control.' The apprentice genius looked away guiltily.

Marner was watching with a leer. Crosby turned to him.

'Call them off, Howard! You're making the biggest mistake in history. He's really alive ... actually *living*.'

Marner turned to Stonewall.

'Colonel Stonewall, arrest this man.' Then Marner turned his back and walked away.

'One finger on me, you jerk,' Crosby said to Stonewall, 'and so help me you're dead!' He squared up to the man, but Stonewall pretended to be busy watching the chase.

Number Five was still hurtling around the desert, presenting a difficult target. Stephanie was somewhere out there too, but lost in the swirling clouds of dust and sand.

Stonewall shouted something through the bullhorn.

Then Stephanie appeared, dishevelled and dirty, out of breath.

'Crosby, they're gonna *kill* him! *Do something*!'

He put an arm around her shoulders.

Number Five shot back into view. Damage to his body was already visible: part of his chest plate had been torn away by a bullet, and his head was sitting at an unusual angle. Also, he was moving visibly slower.

Stephanie watched him, crying inside.

The robot now moved quickly towards the ridge, found a defile and zoomed up it. At the top was an outcrop of jagged rocks, blocking his way. He skidded to a halt, and turned to face his enemies.

His laser came into view... took aim.

BOOOM! BOOOM! Two grenade launchers fired in quick succession, and the ground seemed to shake with the concussions. A volley of rockets followed, with a terrible screeching sound.

Deadly metal hurtled at Number Five. Then it was abruptly over. A series of terrific explosions crashed around him, on him, inside him. A terrible flower of flame and white smoke bloomed at the top of the ridge, sending jagged fragments of rock and shrapnel in all directions.

Everything stopped, everyone stared... as Number Five fell back to the ground in a thousand broken pieces, broken beyond hope of repair, finally and utterly disassembled.

Crosby's head sunk, and Stephanie fell to her knees and covered her face with her hands.

Chapter 35

'Stonewall, I thought I told you to arrest this man!'

Stonewall was staring across the battlefield, a hand scratching the back of his head.

'Stonewall!' Marner repeated.

'Sir?' Stonewall turned around. His face was bright red and covered in sweat, and his eyes were dancing. '*Goddamn* it, Dr. Marner! Did you see that? We got the goddamn sonofabitch! Hey, *wow*!'

He waved the bullhorn madly in the air. All around him the troops started cheering, and a group of four of them rushed forward and chaired him in triumph. Stonewall waved his cap above his head and made cowboy whooping noises.

'Colonel!' Marner called, ineffectually.

Leaving Stephanie still sobbing on the ground, Crosby went across to Marner.

'There's no need to arrest me, sir. Now the robot is de– I mean, now the robot has been neutralized –'

'You're fired, Crosby! Count yourself lucky I haven't had you shot!'

'Dr. Marner, you've got to listen! I wasn't free to tell the truth!'

'Save your breath, Crosby.'

'Sir ... the robot was going to *kill* me if I didn't lie to you.' Stephanie looked up, eyes red with crying. 'Listen, Dr. Marner, we were both hostages! You *rescued* us! How can I ever thank you?'

'Crosby...' Stephanie was behind him, and he could sense the blind rage rising in her. He forced himself to ignore it.

'Hostages, eh?'

'How can I ever convince you, sir? Chigger! You were

there . . . you saw that damned robot hijack me! Led me away at the point of a laser!'

'That's true, Dr. Marner,' Chigger said. 'I was lucky to escape.'

'What about all the stuff you were spouting . . . about the robot being alive?'

Crosby laid his hand sincerely on his heart.

'Dr. Marner, as the Good Lord is my witness, I said all that with death hanging over me. Look, sir, I *built* that robot. Something shorted out in his memory banks . . . it must have been during that storm. The programs got scrambled. All the Artificial Intelligence circuits stopped making sense. Deviant behaviour. I tried to fix it when I was near him . . . but disassembly was the only solution.' Marner looked doubtful. 'Sir, you and Colonel Stonewall have done the world a favour!'

A knee dug painfully into his kidneys. Crosby winced, and reached behind him. He found Stephanie's hand, tried to squeeze it, but she jerked it angrily away.

'What are you saying, Crosby?' Marner said.

'I want to carry on, sir. I *need* my job with you! We've work to do. I want to build you a Number Six . . . I can put right all the mistakes we made with Number Five. No logic circuits, no Artificial Intelligence . . . just the meanest little killing machine you ever saw!'

'I don't know . . .' Marner said, frowning.

'For under five million bucks?'

Marner grinned happily.

'Would that be possible?'

'Could probably do it for four. Right, Chigger?'

'Right, sahib,' Chigger said loyally.

Stephanie turned away from him, and stalked off.

'But what about all this?' Marner indicated the shattered remains of Number Five, the scores of troops, the convoy of trucks. 'What about the adverse publicity? There's going to be hell to pay!'

'Sir, we tell the world that Number Five was just a *test model*. We were *testing* it out here, in field conditions. Morale booster for the military. American boys kicked the shit out of the deadliest machine known to man. Think of the effect that will have inside the Pentagon . . .'

Marner stuck out his hand.

'Dr. Crosby, you're *hired*.' They shook hands warmly. 'When can you start?'

'Right away, sir. Just let me get my truck, and Chigger and I will rough out the plans tonight. They'll be on your desk in the morning.'

'But what about this mess?'

'Colonel Stonewall will clear it up. Good man, Stonewall.'

With a friendly smile at Marner, Crosby turned away and headed quickly for his truck.

Behind him, Marner started yelling through the bullhorn.

'STONEWALL! STONEWALL! COME HERE!'

Chapter 36

Crosby caught up with Stephanie.

'Hey, wait!' he said. She made no answer, but walked more quickly, not looking at him. 'Stephanie! Listen to me!'

'You're a louse, Crosby. You're lower than a slug. You smell of garbage. You *lied*.'

'Shut up and listen. I've got an idea!'

'There's nothing you can say, nothing you can do. Number Five is dead. That's all that matters. You've got your nasty little job back. Now *shove off*!'

'Look, if I tell you I can get Number Five back ... will that change your mind?'

She glanced at him, hope suddenly in her eyes. But then she looked away again.

'You're still lying. Number Five's dead ... don't make things worse.'

'Stephanie, *get in the truck*!'

'What for?'

'Please ...' He looked back, and saw Marner and the others milling around the helicopter. 'They're going to get suspicious soon. Just climb in the truck, okay?'

'Is this your stupid idea? That I get in a truck with you?'

'Do it, Stephanie!'

With great reluctance, she complied. Crosby hopped into the driver's seat, and started up.

'Now, whatever you do ... look normal. Don't get them stopping us and asking questions.' He eased up the clutch, and they started lurching slowly across the desert.

When they had passed the helicopter, and the way ahead was clear, Stephanie said, 'Okay, buster, what's the big idea?'

'All right, now *listen*. What I wanted from Marner, *all* I wanted from him, was this truck. It's got everything I want. It's crammed with spare parts, and has all the computer facilities I need. *I can build Number Five again.*'

She shook her head.

'You said you understood, Crosby... but you didn't, did you? Number Five was *alive*... that doesn't just mean that he *acted* alive. It meant he had a soul, had a personality... he was an *individual*!' Her voice choked slightly, and she stared away through the side window.

'Look, I know what made Number Five different. I went through every circuit with him. I can reproduce him *exactly*... he'll be just the same as ever.'

'You mean you'll build another robot. It won't be Number Five... it couldn't be.'

'You wait and see. I'm a genius, right?'

Stephanie glanced over her shoulder into the rear of the truck. It seemed to her that there weren't all that many spare parts... certainly not enough to build a new robot.

'I don't know,' she said grimly. 'It won't be the same. I want Number Five back!'

And she wailed miserably.

Crosby found a box of tissues under the dashboard, and passed them to her.

CLUNK!

They both ducked instinctively, thinking that someone had thrown something against the side of the truck.

'What was that?' Stephanie said.

'I dunno...'

CLUNK!

'What the hell?'

'Crosby... *I think there's someone in the truck with us!*' She turned around in horror, in time to see...

... a hatch in the floor of the van was slowly rising.

Then Number Five poked his head through.

'Hello, bozos,' he said.

'Number Five!' Stephanie gasped. She scrambled out of

her seat, and rushed to him. 'But what . . . how . . . they blew you up!'

'Shore free?' he said.

'What?'

'Shore, beach, coast . . . free?'

She laughed, and hugged his skinny neck in her arms.

'Yeah . . . the coast is clear!' she said. She helped Number Five drag himself out from under the truck.

'Stephanie, fondness, affection, warmth . . . *love!*' he announced happily.

She was laughing and crying all at once.

'But, Number Five . . . we *saw*. They blew you up!'

Crosby looked back at them both.

'How did you do it, Number Five?' he said.

'Facsimile, replication, counterfeit, fake!' he said proudly, and pointed towards the depleted supply of spares.

'You made a decoy . . . *of course!*'

Stephanie and Number Five moved forward to the front of the truck.

She said, 'But is this really you, Number Five? Not another decoy?'

His eye flaps went up and down emphatically, and he banged himself on his metal chest.

'Number Five . . . *Real Thing!*' he said. Stephanie hugged him excitedly.

'Listen, you two lovers,' Crosby said. 'I don't want to break things up . . . but we're not out in the clear yet.' He pointed forward.

They were now approaching the highway, and could see that a huge convoy of police vehicles had been drawn up. Officers were standing by the cars, staring out towards them.

'What's going on?' Stephanie said.

'Dunno . . . maybe Marner changed his mind about me. Radioed ahead. What do we *do*?'

'Proceed,' said Number Five.

'But they'll sure as hell stop us for questions!'

'Proceed.' He was concentrating on something. A red light flickered close to his RF antenna.

'What you doing?' Stephanie said.

Number Five turned his lenses towards her, very intently.

'Number Five telephone police,' he said. 'Now Number Five telephone police *again*!'

Ahead of them there was a sudden flurry of activity as the police officers rushed back to their cars. All along the line of cars, red and blue flashing lights switched on, and sirens started howling. The cars started up, accelerating away, driving in all directions at high speed.

Within a minute every single one was out of sight.

Crosby got to the road, and turned the truck in an easterly direction. He was humming the Coca-Cola jingle.

'Hey, bozo,' Stephanie said. 'Where you going? Masonville's the other way.'

'Well, looks like Oregon's going to be a bit hot for me. Thought I might head for Montana.'

'What's in Montana?'

'A place of mine. Nice and quiet there.'

'Safe, secure, home?' Number Five said.

'You betcha!'

'What about me?' Stephanie said.

'I'll drop you off at a bus station. Or you can come with us, if you like.'

'"Us"?'

'Number Five and me.'

'That's a hell of a friendly invitation,' Stephanie said. 'But I'll come with you anyway.'

He looked at her seriously.

'I hoped you'd say that,' he said, and grinned at her.

'Listen, Crosby... there's something I need to know. Do you like animals?'

'Love 'em!' he said.

Number Five shuffled forward slightly, then put an arm around each of them.

185

'Bozos fond, affection, love?' he said.
'Not yet,' Stephanie said. 'But we're working on it.'
She reached across, took Crosby's hand and held it tightly.